R.L. STINE'S

GHOSTS OF
FEAR STREET

FRIGHT KNIGHT

—AND —

THE OOZE

R.L. STINE'S

GHOSTS OF
FEAR STREET ®

FRIGHT KNIGHT

— AND —

THE OOZE

TWICE TERRIFYING TALES

ALADDIN
NEW YORK LONDON TORONTO SYDNEY

ALADDIN
An imprint of Simon & Schuster Children's Publishing Division
1230 Avenue of the Americas, New York, NY 10020
This Aladdin paperback edition May 2010
Fright Knight copyright © 1996 by Parachute Press, Inc.
Fright Knight written by Connie Laux
The Ooze copyright © 1996 by Parachute Press, Inc.
The Ooze written by Stephen Roos
All rights reserved, including the right of
reproduction in whole or in part in any form.
ALADDIN is a trademark of Simon & Schuster, Inc., and related
logo is a registered trademark of Simon & Schuster, Inc.
FEAR STREET is a registered trademark of Parachute Press, Inc.
For information about special discounts for bulk purchases, please contact
Simon & Schuster Special Sales at 1-866-506-1949
or business@simonandschuster.com.
The Simon & Schuster Speakers Bureau can bring authors to your live event.
For more information or to book an event contact the Simon & Schuster Speakers
Bureau at 1-866-248-3049 or visit our website at www.simonspeakers.com.
Designed by Karin Paprocki
Manufactured in the United States of America
0410 OFF
2 4 6 8 10 9 7 5 3 1
Library of Congress Control Number 2009931819
ISBN 978-1-4169-9135-9
These titles were previously published individually by Pocket Books.

FRIGHT KNIGHT

"More blood!" I ordered. I slowly stepped back from the guillotine.

I gazed down at the body kneeling at the bottom of the guillotine. His hands were tied behind his back. I spotted the head on the floor, a few feet away.

The blank eyes stared up at me. The mouth gaped open, frozen in a scream of terror.

I walked over and nudged it with the toe of my sneaker.

"This is nowhere near scary enough," I said.

"Right you are, Mike." Mr. Spellman squirted more fake blood on the wax dummy. A long stream of the sticky red stuff dribbled over the gleaming steel blade of the guillotine.

It looked great—just right for the Museum of History's Mysteries.

"Yu-u-uck!" My sister, Carly, let out one of her earsplitting squeals. She'd been so quiet I had almost forgotten she existed.

No such luck.

She started to jump down from her seat on the old mummy case. Salem, our big black cat, leaped off her lap with an angry meow. Then Carly's feet hit the floor.

"You guys are gross!" She gave us the famous Carly look and rolled her eyes.

Carly has the same blue eyes as me. Her hair is shoulder length and mine is buzzed short for the summer. But it's the same hair. Red. We even have the same freckles all over our noses and cheeks.

My dad has red hair, too. In the pictures I've seen, my mother had brown hair and was kind of small, like me. I don't remember our mom at all. She died when we were really little. For as long as I can remember there's just been Dad, Carly, and me.

I'm twelve and Carly is eleven. We're practically the same height, too. A lot of people think we're twins.

It's enough to make a guy hurl.

My dad says not to worry. Girls grow faster than boys. He promised that someday I'll tower over her.

I dream of that day.

"How can you get so excited over something so

2

gross?" Carly shivered. "All that phony blood. It's . . . it's—"

"Terrific!" Dad ran into the room. I could tell that he had been dusting the mummies again. Big gunky cobwebs trailed from his clothes. Clouds of dust puffed out of his red hair.

Dad dashed over to the guillotine. He checked it from every angle. His grin grew wider and wider. "Excellent work!"

Mr. Spellman smiled proudly. He took his job as museum caretaker very seriously. Dad gave me and Mr. Spellman the thumbs-up. "But maybe just a little more blood . . ." he added.

Dad took the plastic bottle and squirted a red puddle all around the head. When he was done, he nodded. "Perfect! It's really horrible now."

"Way to go, Dad," I said.

Carly made a soft gagging sound.

He looked right at her. "Don't forget, scary is exactly why people come to Fear Street." Dad's hands were covered with fake blood. He scratched his ear, and a red glob smeared across his face.

Cool! The blood looked even creepier on a live person than it did on a wax dummy. And it will look totally awesome smeared all over me on Halloween.

"That's why the Museum of History's Mysteries is such a stroke of genius." Dad glanced around the old place and smiled.

"I can't fail. Not this time," Dad vowed. "This is the perfect business for Fear Street. It's why we decided to move here to Shadyside in the first place."

I thought back and remembered—remembered the very night Dad got his great brainstorm to move here and open the museum.

So many weird things happen in Shadyside that the town was on the news almost every night. Dad figured people would want to come here and find out for themselves if the stories were true. Which made it the perfect place for a scary museum.

"Where else could you find ghosts playing hide-and-seek in the cemetery?" Dad asked, thinking back to a recent ghost sighting.

"And don't forget that haunted tree house in the woods," Mr. Spellman added.

Dad sighed. "How could I ever forget that?"

I know Mr. Spellman tries to be helpful. But reminding Dad about my friend Dylan and his haunted tree house only made Dad sad. He had missed out on meeting any of the ghosts and was still sort of bummed out about it.

"All we need is something special that people will be . . . well, dying to see." He chuckled at his own joke. "Then people will come. And the Museum of History's Mysteries will be a big success."

"You mean like the alien tracking station you set up

4

in Grandpa Conway's backyard, Dad?" Carly whined. She didn't give Dad time to answer. She went right on whining.

"Or that freaky petting farm you bought? Let's see—there was the two-headed llama and that stupid unicorn. Couldn't you tell it was a goat with a cardboard horn tied to its head?"

Dad cringed. "I almost forgot about that one," he admitted. "Hey, I thought it was real. Everybody did. It looked real, didn't it, Mike?"

"It looked real to me," I agreed.

Carly made a really mean face at me. I call it her rodent face. It was one of the things she did best.

But I made a better face back at her.

"I think it's going to be great," I said. "All my friends say this place is totally awesome."

"Totally awesome—" Carly imitated me in a squeaky little voice. "Bunch of nerds," she mumbled to herself.

I glared at her. But before I could answer, she turned to my dad again.

"Come on, Dad. What normal kid wants to live in a place that has mummies in the living room and coffins in the dining room and catapults and swords in the kitchen?" she complained.

"How would *you* know what normal kids like, Carly?" I asked.

5

Besides, she wasn't even right. Well, not exactly. All those things were in what used to be the living room and the dining room and the kitchen. That was before Dad turned the downstairs of the big old house into the museum.

We lived upstairs. Our living room, dining room, and kitchen were pretty ordinary compared to down here.

"All right, you two." Dad stepped between us. "No time to fight. Halloween is only two short weeks away. And Shadyside will be crawling with tourists. We've got to be ready for them. We haven't had many customers yet. But Halloween's the perfect time to improve our business." Behind his black-framed glasses Dad's eyes grew serious. I knew what the look meant. He was worried. "They'd better come," he added very quietly. "Or I will have to close."

I knew the thought of closing the museum made Dad sad. It made Mr. Spellman and me sad, too. The Museum of History's Mysteries was a one-and-only kind of place. A place where people could see all sorts of great, spooky stuff. Wax dummies lurked in the basement in the Hall of Wax. Terrifying instruments of torture hung on the back porch. A totally awesome bunch of medieval weapons decorated the front hall. There was no place like it in the whole world.

"Don't worry, Dad," I said. "People will line up and

down the street when that special exhibit gets here from England."

Dad cheered up in a flash. "That's right! Uncle Basil sent it weeks ago. It should be here any day. I can't wait. Imagine how lucky we are! Owning our very own suit of armor!"

I couldn't wait, either. I'm crazy about knights in armor. That was one of the main reasons Mr. Spellman and I were such good friends. He could hardly stop talking about them.

Mr. Spellman worked as the caretaker of the museum since it opened. We have been real close ever since. I couldn't guess his age, but he looked way older than Dad. He was tall and thin. He wore his white hair long, and he had a bushy white mustache. His bright blue eyes lit up whenever he talked about his favorite subjects. Like guillotines or how mummies were made.

He knew everything about really important stuff like that.

Most important, he knew all about knights and swords and castles and dragons.

We talked about knights for hours. He taught me the names of all the weapons—and all about the rules of chivalry. The rules of chivalry told a knight how to behave. How to fight fair. How to be a brave knight.

Mr. Spellman walked over to me and smiled. "And

don't forget," he reminded us, "in his letter, Basil said he was sending along something extra special just for Mike."

Carly didn't need to be reminded. Uncle Basil wasn't sending a present for her.

Her face got all puckery. Like the time we had a contest to see who could eat a whole lemon.

Carly won.

"Aren't you guys forgetting what else Uncle Basil said? That suit of armor is supposed to be haunted!"

"I sure hope so. That's the best thing about it, Carly." Dad wiped the fake blood from his hands with an old rag. "If it is haunted, we're sitting on a gold mine!"

A shiver skipped up my back. The kind of trembly feeling I always felt waiting for something great. My birthday. Or the last day of school.

Or when I felt scared.

But I wasn't scared. I just felt excited. Yeah, that was it. That's why I had a weird, jumpy feeling in my stomach. Sort of like I'd accidentally swallowed a live bug.

"Mr. Conway?" someone called from the front porch. The guy sounded nervous. A lot of delivery and repair people did when they came to the Museum of History's Mysteries. "It's Stanley's Moving and Storage. Got a delivery here for you!"

We all raced out to the front porch. I spotted a giant

8

moving van parked in front of our house. Two delivery men were pulling a huge crate out of the back. I skidded to a stop in the middle of the porch. Carly slammed into my back. She peered over my shoulder to see what was going on.

The wooden crate had a long, rectangular shape. The rough, dark wood looked very old and knotty. A few of the planks were warped and cracked.

I saw strange-looking stamps all over it. The printing on them looked weird, with strange, twisted letters that I could hardly read. But one big stamp that I could read said FRAGILE in bold red letters.

The delivery men tipped the crate on its side to stand it up. It towered over them.

Dad and Mr. Spellman walked all around it. I scrambled over to them. Carly followed me.

The two delivery guys grunted as they hoisted the crate up on their shoulders. From down where I stood, it looked bigger than ever.

"It's the armor, isn't it?" I asked. I peered through the cracks between the planks of wood, but I couldn't see a thing. I hopped up and down. I couldn't help it. Dad didn't have to answer. I knew his answer from the smile on his face.

"Now be careful. Not too fast. Easy does it, fellas." Dad directed them. "Carry it over to the front porch. We'll drag it inside from there. Carly, out of the way. Mike, you'd better be careful. Not so close. You'll—"

Dad's last words vanished in a kind of choking sound as something sliced through the crate. It gleamed in the sunlight.

It was a giant ax. A knight's battle-ax.

And it came right at me.

The huge blade zipped through the air. As if an invisible hand had taken aim. The blade fell down.

I screamed and jumped out of the way.

But not far enough.

2

"**M**y foot! My foot!"

I took a deep breath. I felt like I was going to hurl. Then I moved my foot. I wiggled my toes.

My toes?

I forced myself to look down.

The ax blade stuck into the ground. On one side I saw the white rubber toe of my sneaker. On the other side, I saw the rest of my foot.

"Heh, look—" I moved my foot away from the ax. I poked my toes through the hole in my sneaker and wiggled them wildly. They were still attached. All five of them.

My father sighed. A long sigh of relief. I grinned at him.

"It's just the rubber from the shoe, Dad. My toes are fine."

The battle-ax had sliced off the front of my shoe, but I had pulled back my toes just in time. Lucky break for me.

"You've got to be more careful, Mike." Dad slapped my back in that friendly sort of way he always did when he was worried and he didn't want me to know it. "Why don't you go inside and change your shoes."

I didn't want to. I didn't want to miss a second of the excitement. Before I had a chance to start griping, Mr. Spellman put a hand on my shoulder.

"Come on," he said. "Race you to the house."

That was all I needed to hear. I hurried up the steps to the house. I shot under the sign above the door that said MUSEUM OF HISTORY'S MYSTERIES in creepy-looking red letters on a black background. I shoved open the front door and skidded to the right, all set to bolt up the stairs.

I didn't need to. My old sneakers sat on the landing at the bottom of the steps. Right where I was never supposed to leave them.

Mr. Spellman came huffing and puffing into the house. I already had my chopped-up shoes off. I slipped on my old ones.

"Slower than a snail!"

I always said that to Mr. Spellman when I beat him in a race. He usually laughed.

12

He didn't this time. I don't think he even heard me.

Mr. Spellman looked really excited. His blue eyes lit up. His smile made his bushy white mustache twitch. He plunked down on the step next to me. "Did you see what I saw?" he asked.

He glanced over at the front door. Through the open door we saw Stanley and the other delivery guy coming up the steps with the crate. "Did you read the shipping labels on that crate?"

"Uh, no," I told Mr. Spellman.

"You didn't read them!" he exclaimed in disbelief.

"Give me a break. It's hard to start reading shipping labels when a great big battle-ax is about to split you in two."

"Okay, okay. Those labels say that the armor was shipped from Dreadbury Castle." Mr. Spellman rubbed his hands together. "This is even better than I thought, Mike. Much better."

"It is?"

"If I remember my history right . . ." Thinking really hard, Mr. Spellman squeezed his eyes shut. "Yes. That's right. That's it!" He hopped to his feet. "Dreadbury Castle was the home of Sir Thomas Barlayne!"

He announced the name as if it was supposed to mean something to me.

It didn't.

Mr. Spellman shook his head. "Don't you remember the story of Sir Thomas Barlayne? Sir Thomas was an evil knight. A wicked knight. Some say he was the most wicked knight who ever lived. Finally a noble wizard cast a spell on Sir Thomas. He trapped the wicked knight inside his suit of armor forever."

I stood up. "But that's good, isn't it? That's just what Dad wants. A haunted suit of armor for the museum."

"Yes, that's what your dad wants." Some of the excitement faded from Mr. Spellman's eyes. His voice dropped low. "I wonder if he knows the rest of the story."

He might have been talking to himself, but he sure got my attention.

I grabbed Mr. Spellman's sleeve and tugged. "Rest of what story?"

Mr. Spellman laughed. "Oh, nothing much," he said. He waved away my question with one hand. "It's just some silly old story. According to the legend, whoever owns Sir Thomas's armor is cursed. He's doomed to bad luck—or worse!"

"Worse?" The word squeaked out of me. Bad luck, I could imagine. I could picture getting F's on math tests even though I studied. I could imagine my friend Pete telling the whole world I had a crush on Sara Medlow. And I sure could picture being Carly's brother.

All that was bad luck.

But worse?

"But if the legend is true, won't that be great for the museum?"

Mr. Spellman looked down at me. His eyes twinkled. His mustache twitched. "Maybe not so great for us, huh?"

He bent down so that he could look right into my eyes. "I'll tell you what, Mike. Let's keep this our secret, okay? There's no use worrying your dad. And we don't want to scare Carly. If the armor is haunted . . ."

He straightened up and looked out the window. "What do you say we play detective?"

"You mean we'll check it out together?"

Mr. Spellman nodded.

"Excellent!" He slapped me a high five. "And don't worry, Mr. Spellman," I told him. "I'll watch out for you."

"And I"—Mr. Spellman ruffled my hair—"will watch out for you. Deal?"

"Deal!"

We walked outside onto the porch together. We both smiled about our secret pact. I saw the delivery guys climbing back into their truck. Then I saw the crate stretched out beside me.

Dad didn't waste any time. Holding a crowbar, he crouched down next to the crate. He slipped the edge of the bar under the crate's lid and pushed. I heard a squeaking sound as the nails that held the lid in place came loose.

As Dad pushed up with the crowbar, Mr. Spellman grabbed the edge of the lid and pulled. Carly stood to one side. She was pretending she didn't care much. But I noticed that she was chewing on her lower lip. Her nervous habit.

I sort of hopped around the crate in the circle. I felt so excited I couldn't keep still.

Finally Dad and Mr. Spellman lifted the lid off the crate. I scooted forward. I held my breath. Carly stood right next to me.

We all leaned over and peered inside.

All I saw were piles and piles of fluffy stuff. Shredded newspaper.

"It's paper." Carly sounded as disappointed as I felt.

Dad grinned. "Not just paper, Carly," he said. "Go ahead. Reach in there and see what you can find."

"Me?" Carly squeaked.

"Are you afraid?" Dad asked.

"No way," she said. I could tell she was scared silly. But acting like everything was cool.

The long crate suddenly reminded me of a coffin. I wondered if Carly had the same idea, too.

Her mouth twitched. She pushed up the sleeve of her blue sweater. She reached into the crate. Her arm disappeared into the mountains of paper shreds.

The paper rustled as she felt around for something solid. I saw her lean over and reach in even deeper.

"I think I feel something," she told us.

Then she screamed.

"It's got me! It's grabbed me! Help!"

I watched Carly try and try again to yank her arm out.

But something—or someone—had grabbed her.

And it wouldn't let go.

3

Carly tugged and squirmed. Her face turned red. Dad and Mr. Spellman started digging. Shredded newspaper flew in all directions.

"Hold on now, honey," Dad said.

"Hurry! It's got me," she wailed.

She was out of control. Even I felt sorry for her. Well, almost.

Dad pulled up her arm. The fingers of a metal hand were wrapped around Carly's wrist.

"Well, would you look at this," Dad said. He laughed. The metal hand was attached to a long metal arm.

"Your bracelet got caught," Dad said. "Hold still. I'll have you unhooked in a second." He pried the metal fingers open one by one. Carly snatched back her hand.

The metal hand and arm dropped back into the crate with a clunk.

"Stupid armor," Carly grumbled. She looked down at her wrist, rubbing it.

I looked over my shoulder at Mr. Spellman. I rolled my eyes. He rolled his, too.

Dad reached in and pulled out another piece. "Now look at this," he said.

Smiling, Dad held up a helmet. The last rays of the setting sun glinted against the metal, turning it glowing red. Hot. Fiery.

My mouth fell open. I didn't even realize I was holding my breath until I let it go. "Cool! It's so cool."

Then Dad handed the helmet to me. Just looking at the helmet was nothing compared to touching it.

I ran my hands over it. It felt heavier than I thought it would. And not cold. Not like metal should be. It felt warm. The way it would be if somebody had just taken it off.

A shiver crawled up my back. I cradled the helmet in my arms. Dad pulled a metal shin guard out of the crate and set it on the floor. A metal foot guard came next.

Dad's eyes gleamed. He reached into the pile of shredded paper for another piece of the armor. "This is it! Our chance at fame and fortune. This is going to be the best and the spookiest exhibit anyone has ever seen. On Fear Street or any place else. People will come from all over the world to see it and—"

His words stopped suddenly. His sandy-colored eyebrows drew together as he frowned. He kept moving his hand around under the shredded paper. He felt around for something way down at the bottom of the crate.

"What's this?" Dad pulled his arm out. He held up something bright and shiny. The strange round object dangled at the end of a long golden chain.

It looked like a giant marble, but weirder looking than any marble I had ever seen.

Inside the marble strange blue smoke spiraled and swirled. Dark blue. Light blue. Sparkling silvery flecks whirled slowly around in the smoke, like tiny shooting stars.

I grabbed for it.

So did Carly.

So did Mr. Spellman.

I got there first.

"Slower than snails!" I grinned at them, the pendant in my hands. "This must be my special surprise from Uncle Basil!" I slipped the chain over my neck before anybody else had a chance to touch it. I stared down at the pendant dangling against my white T-shirt. "Gee—it looks cool, doesn't it?"

Dad agreed. So did Carly. She sounded jealous. That made me like the pendant even more.

Mr. Spellman stepped forward. "If you ask me," he said, looking at the pendant, "it looks positively magical."

"Yeah, it does sort of, doesn't it?" I nodded.

A magic pendant.

It was the best surprise I'd had since Dad took us to New York City last year to buy a new mummy.

We all watched as Dad finished unpacking the crate. We gathered up the armor and took it into the front hall.

Mr. Spellman and I handed Dad the pieces. Piece by piece, he slowly put Sir Thomas together.

Carly stood by, holding Salem in her arms. I could tell she didn't want to touch the armor.

When Dad finished, we all stood back and took a good look.

Sir Thomas's armor could have easily fit my favorite pro wrestler, Hulk Hooligan. The shoulders were about a yard wide. The legs were round and solid. They reminded me of small tree trunks. About three of me could have hidden behind the breastplate, no problem.

I thought about all the stories in all my books about castles and knights.

"Awesome!" I let out the word at the end of a sigh.

"He does look awesome, doesn't he?" Mr. Spellman clapped me on the back.

Dad smiled. "Now all we have to do is keep our fingers crossed. If we're lucky, this old pile of metal really is haunted. And that will bring the customers running!"

The phone rang and Dad went to answer it. Mr. Spellman hurried out, too. He said he had some work to do down in the wax museum. When they were gone, Carly edged up real close to me.

"What do you think, Mikey?" She always calls me Mikey when she tries to make me mad. "Are you scared the armor might really be haunted?"

"The only thing I'm scared of is your ugly face!" I gave her a playful punch on the arm. Then I dashed out of the hall and up the stairs.

It was my turn to start dinner. I knew exactly what I was going to make—macaroni and cheese, the food Carly hated more than anything in the whole wide world.

It was Carly's turn to do the dishes. I made sure I cooked the macaroni and cheese just a little too long. So after dinner she had to scrape all the hard pieces off the bottom of the pan. While she was doing that and grumbling to herself, I hurried to my room.

I still had a school project to do about polar bears. I had to read the report to my class tomorrow. Also my favorite TV show, *Scream Theater,* was on at nine.

I did my homework, but I never got a chance to watch *Scream Theater.* It had been a big day. I was beat.

I brushed my teeth, pulled on my pajamas, and fell into bed.

But I kept my pendant on. Stretched out in bed, I held it up in front of my face. I watched the curling blue smoke glimmer in the moonlight that slipped through my window blinds.

I got this weird feeling that the smoke was hiding something. Something really great. I tried to get a closer look. But the more I looked, the more the color swirled.

I fell asleep before I knew it.

Thump. Thump.

I was dreaming about something. I couldn't remember what. I thought it had something to do with polar bears. And blue marbles. And knights in shining armor.

Thump. Thump.

There it was again.

I opened my eyes and listened.

Thump. Thump.

Definitely not part of my dream.

I sat up and held my breath.

23

Thump. Thump.

It came from downstairs.

Thump. Thump.

I swung my legs over the side of the bed. I sat with my head tilted, listening closer.

Thump. Thump.

I couldn't think of anything down in the museum that made that kind of noise.

At least, not before tonight.

Thump. Thump.

I stood up. My legs felt a little rubbery.

Only one thing could be making the noise.

The armor.

Thump. Thump.

I gulped and hurried downstairs. The museum kitchen was right under my room. The closer I got to it, the louder it sounded.

Thump. Thump.

I gazed down at my pendant. The swirling blue smoke pulsed to the rhythm of the sounds.

Thump. Thump.

I moved through the museum, following the sound. At the door to the kitchen, I stopped. I gulped for air, the way I do in gym class when Mr. Sirk, our PE teacher, makes us run extra laps.

This was it! My chance to catch a ghost in action. My chance to prove that the armor really was haunted!

Thump. Thump.

I took a deep breath. I pushed open the kitchen door.

Thump. Thump.

I took a couple of shaky steps inside.

Thump. Thump.

I squinted into the dark. And I saw it.

It was hideous.

I couldn't help it. I screamed.

4

"Carly! You creep!"

My jerky sister stood in the middle of the kitchen with a broom in her hands. She pounded on the ceiling with the handle.

I glared at her. "What do you think you're doing?" I tried to keep my voice down. I didn't want to wake Dad.

Carly was doubled over laughing. She pointed at my face. "Look, it's the nerd patrol. Out ghost hunting."

Carly laughed some more. She can really crack herself up with her dumb jokes.

"Yeah, well, only a true jerk starts banging a broom handle on the ceiling in the middle of the night," I said.

I fingered my blue pendant. Now that the thumping had stopped, the pulsing had stopped, too. I closed my fingers around it.

"You're lucky Dad didn't wake up," I told her. "He would have thought the ghost had come for sure. He would have been so excited. Can you imagine how he would have felt when he found out it was only you?"

For once, Carly actually looked sorry. She put down the broom. "I guess I never thought of that," she said. "I just wanted to scare you."

"Well, you didn't." I crossed my arms over my chest. I tried to give her the same kind of look Dad gave us when we made him angry or disappointed. "You just caused trouble, that's all."

I suppose I should have considered myself lucky. I had actually seen Carly look sorry for once. I should have known it would never happen again.

"What's the matter, Mikey? Were you afraid of the big, bad knight down here?"

"Look who's talking. You're the one who thought it grabbed you," I reminded her. "O-o-oh! Help me! Help me!" I imitated her in a high-pitched, girl voice.

"Well, I'm not scared now," she said. She tossed her hair over one shoulder. "You're the one who believes in haunted armor."

"Well, what if the legend is true?" I asked her. "Do you want to meet the ghost of the most wicked knight who ever lived?"

"Oh, come on," Carly said. "You don't believe all that stuff? I mean, you don't think the armor could . . . could walk around or anything, do you?"

"There's only one way to find out."

Carly pretended that she didn't care about the haunted armor and the curse. But I could tell that deep down inside, she was scared.

But I wasn't scared.

"Come on." I grabbed her arm and pulled her out of the kitchen. "Let's go check it out."

As we left the kitchen and turned down the dark hallway, I started to get that creepy feeling again.

Not that I'm a chicken or anything. But the Museum of History's Mysteries can be sort of spooky. Especially at night.

In the moonlight that poured through the windows, our shadows looked all twisted and deformed. And things around the place you normally didn't notice, like a lamp or a big potted plant, looked a lot different in the dark—like they might reach out and grab you.

I heard a *squeak, squeak, squeak.* It sounded like fingernails on a blackboard. It made my skin crawl.

I stopped.

The noise stopped.

It was only the floor. I sighed.

I should have known. Everything around the museum always squeaks. It's part of what makes the big old house so much fun.

28

Except at night. When you're creeping through the place all alone with no one but your goofy sister. And you're looking for a haunted suit of armor.

We reached the dining room, where Dad's entire coffin collection is on display. He likes to call the room Coffin Central. He thinks that's pretty funny.

In the daytime it's a great place to play hide-and-seek.

But at night . . .

I heard a small hiccup. Then I realized I had made it. I glanced over at Carly, waiting for her to tease me.

But for once, Carly didn't say a word. I guess the room had creeped her out, too. She grabbed my hand. Her steps dragged.

I pulled her into the room. All the coffins were closed. Mr. Spellman always closed them before he went home at night.

What did it matter? Both of us knew what each and every one of them held.

The one next to us held a wax dummy of Dracula. Wooden stake through the heart and all.

The one over on our right had a wax dummy inside, too.

But the dummy had a mirror in place of a face. When you bent over the coffin and looked inside . . .

A shiver snaked its way up my back and over my shoulders. I walked a little faster.

"You're not scared, are you, Mikey?" This time

Carly wasn't teasing me. I could tell she was hoping I'd say no.

"No way." Was that me talking so tough? I tried to keep my voice steady. "There's nothing to be afraid of—

"Yow!" I let out a yelp of pain. Carly grabbed my arm.

"Mike? What? What?"

"I banged my knee on a coffin." Ouch. I rubbed my leg. "That hurts."

"Try not to be such a klutz," she whispered. "You'll wake up Dad."

"Try not to be such a chicken."

"Me? I'm not afraid of anything," she said.

"Except the haunted armor," I reminded her.

I kept walking, but Carly stopped in her tracks. I glanced back at her. She stood frozen to the spot. She peered into the shadows, twisting a strand of hair with her fingers.

"Maybe this isn't such a great idea after all. I mean . . ." Carly said in a shaky voice, "what if there really is a ghost? Maybe we should give him a few nights to sort of rest and get used to the place."

I didn't bother answering. Mostly because I hoped there *was* a ghost. And a curse. I wanted people to come to see Sir Thomas from miles around so we would make a zillion dollars and could live in the museum forever.

We finally made it through the coffin room and went into the living room. Even though Dad had spent the entire afternoon dusting the mummies, dust covered every inch of everything else. Clouds of dust drifted over the floor and blew around our feet as we walked.

That's exactly the way Dad likes it.

Dusty and musty. With cobwebs hanging off the walls like ghoulish party streamers.

As we crept across the floor, our slippers made a dull scraping sound. The sound a mummy might make dragging itself across the room.

Mr. Spellman always closed the coffins at night. But the mummies were always open for business.

Out of the corner of my eye I could see Dad's favorite mummy. The one he called Charlie. Charlie stood propped up in his case. His stiff arms jutted out in front of him. His sunken eyes stared across the darkness. Right at us.

I made a gulping sound and tried to cover it up with a cough.

"Race you the rest of the way!" I dropped Carly's hand. I sprinted into the parlor. Dad had set up the armor on a wooden stand just inside the doorway.

I beat Carly by a mile and stopped near the open door, waiting for her.

Finally she caught up. I grinned. "Slow as a snail!"

Carly didn't answer.

She stared over my shoulder. Her mouth dropped open.

She pointed.

I looked through the doorway and saw—nothing.

Empty space.

The armor was gone!

5

"**M**ike!" Carly's voice trembled. "Mike, where is he? Where is the knight?"

He had vanished all right. All that remained of him was his wooden stand.

"Do you know what this means?" I asked her.

"Yeah." Carly gulped. "The armor moved. It really is haunted."

"Right! The story is true!" I whispered. "Sir Thomas's ghost is in that armor. And he can move! He can walk!"

"He could be anywhere!" Carly croaked. "He could be hiding in the basement. He could be on his way upstairs." She took a step back into the mummy room. "He could be right in this room. Hiding in the dark."

I scanned the shadows. "I don't think so," I told her. "He's pretty big. I think we'd notice him. Let's look for him."

"Maybe he'll come back on his own," she replied in a shaky voice. "Like Salem does when he sneaks out of the house at night."

"Carly, get real. We're talking about a ghost, okay?"

I grabbed a handful of her robe and dragged her back the way we came. We already knew Sir Thomas wasn't in the mummy room. He wasn't in the coffin room. I didn't look too closely at the dark shadows in the kitchen, but I felt pretty sure he wasn't in there, either.

"Let's check out the wax museum."

"No way!" Carly hates the wax museum. She squinched up her eyes. "Anywhere but the wax museum!"

"All right." I paused and thought about where a ghost might be lurking. "How about the conservatory?"

Before Carly could think of some dumb excuse, I led her toward the back of the house.

When we first moved into the house on Fear Street, it took me a long time to figure out what a conservatory was. Dad finally explained that it was a sort of greenhouse. The huge, empty, roller rink-size room had a glass ceiling and glass walls on one end. The original owners of the house used to grow all kinds of plants in there, even in the winter.

Dad hardly ever used the conservatory for museum exhibits. It was way too big. And really needed some repairs.

We pushed open the door and went inside. Eerie blue moonlight shone down through the glass walls and domed roof.

We crept along, close to the wall, and then ducked under the tropical plants Dad planned to use in the mummy exhibit. I peered through the big, floppy leaves. Something up ahead flashed and sparkled.

Like moonlight glinting off armor.

With one finger on my lips, I signaled Carly to keep quiet. We tiptoed through the shadows side by side. A cobweb trailed across my face. I brushed the sticky web aside. And caught my breath.

Sir Thomas! There he was.

He sat on a full-size model horse, right in the middle of the conservatory. The high glass dome arched above him.

I blinked.

For a second I thought I saw him move.

I blinked again.

I took a step closer.

"Awesome!" My voice echoed in the big empty room.

A high ladder stood next to the model horse. The ladder Dad always used to set up his exhibits.

"See? You were scared for nothing." I knew I didn't have to whisper anymore. "Dad and Mr. Spellman must have done it. They must have moved the knight in here when we were doing our homework."

I noticed then that they had also moved most of Dad's medieval weapons in here, too. Almost his entire collection. About a dozen lances hung on the wall to the left of the knight. And on the wall to the right of the knight I saw a display of big metal swords and shields.

Propped up in the corner, I spotted Dad's fake suit of armor, too. He'd bought it for a display in the museum and it had all the details of real armor. It even looked real from a distance. But close up you could tell it was made of cheap, thin tin.

I'd always loved that fake armor. But now that we had the real thing, it didn't look like much.

"Looks like they brought a lot of stuff in here," I said.

Carly wrinkled her nose. "Why?"

"Why?" A Carly question if I ever heard one. "Probably because there's more room in here. More people will have a chance to see the armor and all the cool weapons a knight like Sir Thomas needed to fight his enemies."

I stared up at Sir Thomas again. "He's awesome, isn't he?"

"Yeah, awesome," she echoed halfheartedly.

Seated on the horse, Sir Thomas appeared ready to fight. He carried a long, pointy lance in one hand. His other hand wrapped around the horse's reins. In that same hand he also grasped a shield.

The ghostly white moonlight flickered off Sir Thomas's helmet. It sparkled against his lance. It made the armor glow with a powerful green light. Glow from the inside.

It was the coolest thing I ever saw in my whole, entire life. I wanted to get as close as I could. Really, really close.

I walked toward him.

"Mike, what are you doing?"

Over my shoulder I saw Carly take a step back. "Dad might not like it if you—"

"Dad won't mind."

Oh, yes, he would, a little voice inside said. *He'd mind big-time. You'll be grounded for the rest of your life if he catches you messing around with that armor.*

But I'm not going to mess with it, I answered the voice. *I only want a closer look. Just one tiny peek. I've got to see where that green glow is coming from. Dad will understand.*

"It's truly excellent, isn't it?"

I don't know if Carly answered me or not. I wasn't listening.

All of a sudden I had to touch the armor.

I stood really close now. I stretched up as far as I could. That didn't help much. Sir Thomas sat on his horse. And the horse stood on a platform. Like I said, I'm sort of short.

Hey, but that's what ladders are made for, right? I grabbed the ladder and started climbing up.

"Mike, you're not going to—"

I ignored Carly. I ignored everything. Everything but the weird feeling that traveled down my arms. Tingling in my fingers.

I climbed to the very top of the ladder.

From up there the armor looked better than ever. I caught my breath. I studied the fancy designs on the breastplate and helmet. There were even a couple dents. I figured Sir Thomas got those in battle.

I gazed at the visor. The part the knight raised so he could eat and talk.

I gazed into the slit above the visor. The space where the knight looked out. It looked dark and empty.

I hooked my left arm around one side of the ladder. Then I leaned out as far as I could. My fingers brushed Sir Thomas's helmet.

The tingling got stronger.

"See. Nothing to worry about." I glanced down. Carly stared up at me. Her eyes were round. Her mouth hung open. "I bet I can even get a look inside."

Stretching out really far, I hooked my finger around the bottom of Sir Thomas's visor. I nudged it open.

The visor squeaked.

It didn't squeak like the museum floor squeaked. That was a friendly kind of squeak.

This squeak made my bones vibrate. It made my teeth ache.

The ladder wobbled. I steadied myself.

Before I even realized it, I stood face-to-face with the helmet.

Nothing to see. Nothing but a blackness. Blacker than the night.

I leaned over farther and peered inside. Blackness. Thick, dense.

I caught a whiff of something putrid—a pile of old garbage that had been around awhile. Say, a few centuries.

I felt sick to my stomach.

Then I heard a long groan. Like someone moaning from the other end of a long tunnel.

The sound grew louder. It filled my head. It drowned out the noisy *whoosh* of the blood rushing in my ears.

I leaned back and felt the ladder wobble under me. My entire body broke out in gooseflesh.

Something was moving. Inside the helmet. Something was coming. A black shadow!

The shrieking and moaning grew louder. And louder.

The armor trembled. Then shook violently.

With a ghastly cry that chilled my bones, the shadow rose up out of the armor.

I was done for.

6

The shadow rose out of the armor and came straight at me.

With my eyes squeezed shut, I heard a creepy sound of fleshy wings flapping around my head and neck.

I swatted wildly at the air. Then it flew around my head and dived at me from the other side.

I tried to duck. Too late.

The biggest, blackest, ugliest bat that ever lived flew right into my face.

I stared into two terrifying glowing red eyes. The bat's horrid mouth opened, baring sharp fangs. I saw its wicked claws flex. Ready—ready to dig into me.

I swung my arms over my head as the bat swooped at me again. Big, creepy wings flapped against my ear.

"Whoa!" I yelped. I lost my balance and fell backward off the ladder.

I landed on the floor with a thud. I felt like a bug hitting a car windshield.

"Are you all right?" I looked up and saw Carly standing over me. She offered me a hand up.

With a loud grunt I pulled myself to my feet. All my bones seemed to be in one piece. But just barely. I'd lost one of my slippers, and my pajamas had twisted all around my legs.

"Have a nice flight?" Carly asked sweetly.

"Very funny." I dusted off the seat of my pajamas. I spotted my missing slipper over by Sir Thomas's horse. I grabbed it and slipped it on. "That bat had to weigh at least fifty pounds. Its wings stretched out about a yard."

Carly made a face. "Bats! Yuck! Where did it go? Is it still here?" She covered her head and stared at the ceiling.

"I don't know," I said. "It just flew away."

Carly glanced at the ceiling again. "I don't know about you, but I'm going back to bed."

"Go ahead." I stepped back to let her by.

I watched Carly quickly walk out of the conservatory. She disappeared into the shadows on the far side of the room. A minute later I heard the sounds of her footsteps as she climbed the stairs.

42

I sighed. It was late. I had school tomorrow. First thing in the morning I had to give my report. I hoped I didn't nod out right in the middle of it.

Staying up suddenly seemed like a huge waste of time.

Had I found a ghost?

No.

All I found was my stupid sister.

And a bat.

I sighed. Pretty disappointing. I headed for the door. My slippers scuffed across the floor.

But about halfway across the room I thought I saw something. Out of the corner of my eye.

Something moving.

Metal flashing in the moonlight.

I stopped and squinted through the shadows at the armor.

Wasn't Sir Thomas staring in the *other* direction the last time I looked at him?

I shook my head. I rubbed my eyes.

No. Couldn't be.

Right?

The question tapped at my brain. My insides suddenly quivered. I decided to get out of the conservatory. Fast.

My racing footsteps slapped against the tile floor.

My heart pounded against my ribs.

At the door I quickly glanced back at Sir Thomas. He was right where he belonged.

I let out a deep breath and started the long trek to the stairs.

I crept through the kitchen, finding my way by the light of the moon. A cold, spooky glow flowed through the windows.

The moonlight shimmered against a huge, old broadsword hanging on the wall. Next to the sword hung a set of heavy chains. The links looked like teeth.

Hungry teeth. Grinning at me.

I couldn't help it. I shivered.

Get a grip, I told myself. You're acting like a dweeb. A total nerd. This is the Museum of History's Mysteries, right? It's home, right? What are you scared of?

I didn't stop to answer myself. I just walked a little faster.

The coffin room looked exactly the way we had left it.

Or did it?

The lid on Dracula's coffin . . . I didn't remember it being open like that. Just a tiny crack.

I didn't stop to check it out. I dashed into the mummy room.

I saw good old Charlie. Right where he always stood. His eyes still stared their mummy stare. His arms still jutted out straight. Mummy fingers dangling.

Reaching for me as I rushed past.

A flutter in the pit of my stomach told me not to think about that.

But by then it was too late.

My head whirled. I took a deep breath.

And choked on a mouthful of mummy dust.

I needed fresh air. Fast.

I bolted out of the mummy room. Up ahead I saw the doors that led out of the museum. The doors in the parlor. I sprinted toward them, coughing and gasping.

Air. I needed air.

The doors are the big, double kind. The kind they have at school. They have those metal handles that you press down to open. I grabbed the door handle and pressed.

The door didn't move.

I tried again. I pushed against it with my whole body.

Nothing. The door didn't budge an inch.

I dragged my hand over the wall. I felt the light switch and flicked on the overhead lights. Something told me I wasn't going to like what I saw.

My breath caught in my throat. It was a knight's sword.

Someone had jammed it right through both sets of door handles.

I threw myself against the doors and pulled and pulled at the sword. It was heavy. It didn't budge.

I was trapped!

7

"**T**rapped."

I heard my voice echo in the emptiness all around me.

I stood up again and wrapped both my hands around the cold, hard handle of the sword. I took a deep breath and pulled again.

Harder and harder.

My arms ached and blood pounded in my head.

No use.

Panting, I beat the sword with my fists.

Nothing.

I backed up and gave the door and the sword a ninja kick.

My foot throbbed with pain. But the sword didn't even jiggle.

Trapped.

This time the word echoed inside my head.

I had to backtrack. Through the entire museum. Through the mummy room. The coffin room. And the creepy kitchen.

I had to go through the conservatory. I had to reach the back door at the far side of that room. Or else . . .

I stopped myself from thinking that far. I didn't want to think about the evil knight. Not now.

"I can't be trapped. I can't be trapped. I can't be trapped."

I chanted the words out loud as I ran through the dark shadowy rooms.

"How could I be trapped? Carly went out that way. Just a couple minutes ago. There's no way anyone could have stuck that sword in the door since then. I would have seen them. Sure. Yeah. That's right. No way. I would have seen them for sure."

I kept walking and talking out loud to myself. And I hung on to my blue marble pendant. I'm not sure why. But I felt better when I was holding it. Braver.

I stopped at the conservatory door. I opened it a crack and peeked inside.

Sir Thomas was still there—sitting on his horse. Just like when I left him.

I didn't breathe a sigh of relief. I don't think I

breathed at all. The whole time. I held my breath as I brushed under Dad's weird plants. I held my breath as I hurried past the ladder.

When I got all the way past Sir Thomas and nothing happened, I finally let the breath go. I didn't slow down, but the knots in my stomach loosened up a little.

The back door loomed closer. And closer. I walked faster. And faster. It came closer still.

Almost in reach now.

Then I heard a strange sound.

A creaking sound.

Shivers raced up my arms and legs. My knees wobbled.

I told myself, "Keep walking. Do *not* turn around and look."

The creaking grew louder.

But I had to look. I couldn't stop myself.

I turned very slowly.

What I saw made me freeze in place. My heart stopped.

The suit of armor.

Standing right behind me. Towering over me.

How did it get off the horse?

I took a gulp of air and forced myself to look up.

Through the slit above the visor I saw a fiery red glow. When my gaze met that glow, it grew brighter. Hotter. Redder.

Then I knew.

Sir Thomas. He was in there.

The armor creaked as he took a step closer.

I felt myself stumbling backward. The room spun.

"I . . . I . . . I . . ." I sputtered, trying to stay on my feet. Never taking my gaze off him for a second.

Then with the scraping sound of metal against metal, Sir Thomas raised one hand. He pointed right at me.

I stopped sputtering. My mouth hung open.

"You!" His deep voice boomed from inside the suit of armor. "You will not escape me this time, evil wizard!"

8

"**M**e? A wizard?" I choked out the words.

"Wait a second," I sputtered. "I'm just a sixth grader at Shadyside Middle School. Ask anybody. I'm no wizard."

"Save your wizard's lies for fools!" Sir Thomas's words boomed all around me.

The glass dome above us rattled and groaned, as if blasted by a huge gust of wind.

"It is your doing, wicked one. You and your magic trapped me in this metal tomb with your evil magic."

"Me?" I shook from head to toe. My pendant swung back and forth across my chest. The blue smoke inside it swirled.

"You've got me mixed up with somebody else. Honest. I've never even seen you before today, Sir Thomas. Sir Thomas, sir, I mean—" I added. Grownups usually like it when you act all polite. I figured it was worth a try.

No such luck.

"Vile one!" he roared. The fire behind Sir Thomas's visor grew bloodred and flickered. He tilted his head to take a closer look at me.

The next second I heard a furious snarl. Moving way faster than a guy should have been able to move wearing a couple hundred pounds of armor, Sir Thomas raised his lance. He lunged at me. He held the point of it right at my throat. "Prepare to die, hateful wizard!"

The needle-sharp lance pricked my skin. The metal felt fiery hot.

He wanted to kill me.

Slice me in half.

Chop me up in little pieces. And then even smaller pieces after that.

I didn't stand a chance against him.

I swallowed hard and took a giant step back.

Sir Thomas rattled forward. He snarled again. The flames behind his visor flickered and hissed.

"Did you think you could fool me by taking the shape of a young boy?" Sir Thomas roared at me. "I fought you when you turned yourself into a dragon. I fought you when you changed yourself into a wall of fire. And now . . ."

The knight dug the lance tip into my skin. "Now, wizard, I will have my revenge!"

I tried to scream for help. I tried to scream for Dad. Or even Carly.

I croaked pathetically.

Sir Thomas dipped his head and made a deep metallic grinding sound.

I took a couple of steps back.

The knight took a couple steps forward. He tossed his lance away. It clattered to the floor.

Great! He finally believes me, I thought.

Then he stepped even closer.

"I have waited centuries for this moment, wizard. I want to see your evil eyes as you gasp for your dying breath," his deep voice bellowed.

I stared up at him, frozen with fear. I couldn't move. I backed toward a corner. No place to hide. And I knew I'd never get past him alive.

Dad had set up a whole bunch of medieval weapons around the horse. Too bad for me. Sir Thomas had his pick.

"Should I use the broadsword?" Sir Thomas grabbed for it. "Or the mace?" He picked up the mace in his other hand.

He swiped the big, heavy sword through the air. In the moonlight the sharp blade gave off an icy glint.

Then he held out the mace at arm's length.

Sir Thomas's mace looked like a big club. Studded with spikes all around the top. Metal spikes filed to needle-sharp points.

They sparked at me. They flashed.

I cringed. I imagined what they would feel like biting into my skin.

"Chivalry!" I screamed the word. I forced myself to sound brave.

"You call yourself a knight? A real knight wouldn't attack an unarmed person. A real knight wouldn't go against the code of chivalry. Mr. Spellman said so."

The red glow behind the visor flickered.

"You are correct, foul wizard," Sir Thomas admitted. "I cannot attack an unarmed man." He stepped back and swept his arm out over Dad's display of weapons. "Choose."

My hands shaking, my heart pumping, I looked over the weapons. Could I save myself with any of them? Not likely. I picked up a heavy shield. One big enough to hide behind. I clutched it in both hands and ducked in back of it.

Great, I thought.

But not good enough for Sir Thomas.

"Choose!" he roared again.

His command made the conservatory windows rattle.

I dodged out from behind the shield long enough to grab the handle of a mace.

I held the shield in my left hand. I balanced the mace in my right. They weighed about a ton each and my arms ached just trying to hold on to them. How could I ever fight?

Would I even get a chance to try?

Sir Thomas threw his head back and laughed.

The battle had begun.

Lucky for me, I'm fast when I have to be. Even in reverse. My feet skidded on the tile floor as I slid backward. I peered over the top of the shield. I saw Sir Thomas pull his mace back, over his head. Then swing it toward me.

The pointy spikes glistened as the mace streaked through the air. I yelped and pushed the shield up in front of me. I ducked my head and braced myself.

Direct hit.

My bones shook as the mace crashed into my shield. A shower of sparks flew off the shield.

And then I heard a horrible cracking sound.

I knew it meant only one thing.

My crumbling shield wouldn't last much longer.

I squeezed my eyes shut.

Sir Thomas had won.

9

I held my breath. I counted my pounding heartbeats. I knew they'd be my last.

In two seconds I'd be face-to-face with the evil knight. With no shield to protect me.

One. Two. Two and a half.

Two and three-quarters . . .

Nothing happened.

I opened one eye. I opened my other eye.

I checked out my shield. Not a crack in sight.

I spotted Sir Thomas a few steps in front of me. He stared down at his mace.

I stared at it, too.

What remained of it.

When it struck my shield, Sir Thomas's mace

shattered into about a million little pieces. The sharp metal spikes scattered all over the floor.

While Sir Thomas looked closer at the ruined weapon, I peered at the front of my shield. The mace had made a big dent in it, all right. But nothing more.

"Wow!" I couldn't believe my luck.

What was going on here?

Sir Thomas snarled. The red glow behind his visor flared. He hurled his useless mace into the corner. "Wow?" he mimicked. "Do not try your magic words on me, vile creature!"

I spotted his broadsword, gripped in his other metal hand. He sliced the air with some practice swipes as he stomped toward me. The long silver blade flashed in the darkness.

I ducked down and ran for it.

Go! Go! Go! I urged myself.

I couldn't get out the conservatory door. Sir Thomas was blocking it. I pounded through the conservatory. Toward the kitchen. Sir Thomas pounded the floor one step behind me. I threw down the heavy shield. My legs pumped until every muscle ached. My breath burned in my throat.

I heard him close behind me. Closing the small gap. I imagined him reaching out a long metal arm and snagging me by the neck.

I ran even harder.

I punched the door open and raced into the kitchen. My slippers skidded on the tile floor. My feet flew out from under me.

I flailed my arms, trying to keep my balance. Too late. With a painful thud, I landed on my belly and kept sliding.

I heard Sir Thomas's sword whiz through the air above me.

Right where my head would have been.

Our kitchen has one of those islands in it. The kind of counter that stands in the middle of the floor. Regular people use it to cook and serve food. Dad uses it for cleaning weapons.

Scuttling like a beetle, I crawled behind the island. I hopped to my feet and darted to the other end of it, just beyond Sir Thomas's reach.

From my side of the counter I stared over at the knight. The space behind Sir Thomas's visor glowed with bloodred fire. Angry orange sparks shot out from the center of the crackling flames.

What could I use to fight him? I frantically scanned the room. The chains hanging on the wall? Too far away. The broadsword hanging beside them? Too heavy for me even to lift.

Then I saw it.

The catapult.

It stood between me and the door. I could dart over to it and take cover before I dived for the door.

If I could make my feet move.

Fear rooted me to the floor. I felt numb. Paralyzed.

Sir Thomas knew it. The fire in his eyes blazed. He raised his broadsword and whacked it down.

I darted out of the blade's path. Just in time.

The huge blade sliced clean through the countertop.

I crouched behind the catapult and gasped for breath.

With a growl Sir Thomas yanked his sword out of the counter. He swung it from side to side.

With his armor creaking and rattling, he marched toward me.

I could either die here behind the catapult or make one last, desperate dash for the door.

I spun around, all set to go for it.

My hand hit the lever that operated the catapult.

I heard a *boing*ing sound and a *whoosh*. Dad kept a papier-mâché rock in the catapult. I watched it sail toward the knight. I knew it couldn't hurt him, but maybe it would distract him long enough for me to sneak out the door.

It struck him square in the chest.

I dashed to the door. But out of the corner of my eye I saw Sir Thomas stagger back. His arms flew up from his sides. His broadsword and shield clattered to the floor.

The knight raised his head. He looked right at me. The fire in his eyes exploded like lava in a volcano.

Then he fell back onto the floor with a terrible crash.

Knocked out cold.

10

Knocked out? From a papier-mâché rock?

No way.

I came out from behind the catapult really slowly. I stared down at him.

His motionless legs and one arm stuck out from his body at weird angles. His other arm had dropped near the door.

His helmet was tilted to one side. I peered into the slit above his visor but saw only a cold black shadow.

Right in the middle of his breastplate I saw a huge dent.

The knots in my stomach untied. I dragged in a deep breath. It felt like the first one I'd taken in hours.

I spotted the rock under the kitchen table and picked it up. Light as a feather. As always.

A papier-mâché rock couldn't knock out a knight in heavy armor.

But it did!

And I beat the ghastly ghost!

"Yes! Way to go!" I cheered out loud for myself.

"He's lean. He's mean. He's Mike Conway! Undefeated champion—" I announced in my sportscaster's voice.

"Mike?" Dad called from the hallway. He came into the kitchen with Carly. "What's going on down here? Why aren't you in bed?"

Before I could get a word out, Dad flipped on the light.

He gasped. His face turned white. He stared down at the mess of armor on the floor. His mouth hung open.

Then he looked at me.

What a look!

Sir Thomas hadn't killed me. But it looked as if Dad wanted to. Real bad, too.

"Michael Conway! Didn't I tell you to keep your hands off that armor?"

"Now, wait a second, Dad. It's not what you think—"

"It was the bats," Carly piped up. She had on her I-told-you-so face. She crossed her arms over her chest.

"I told you about the bats, Dad. Mike was so afraid of them, he probably ran all over the place, knocking everything over. Including the armor."

"Shut up, Carly. What do you know?" I said. "It was Sir Thomas, Dad," I tried to explain. "He was chasing me all over the place. He called me a wizard. He tried to smash me with his mace, and then he chased me with his sword—" I was speed talking, but I couldn't stop. I wasn't even sure if Dad understood a word I was saying.

"And then, he—"

Suddenly Dad didn't look so sleepy anymore. Behind his glasses, his eyes opened wide.

"The knight? It was him?" Dad grabbed my shoulders. I stopped talking and took a breath. "He made that racket?"

I nodded wildly. Finally he heard me.

"That's wonderful!" Dad said.

"No, Dad. You don't understand."

"You mean he's really haunted?" He stared down at Sir Thomas again. He scooped up the arm that had fallen near the door. He waved it in the air. "What news! What wonderful news! Kids, do you know what this means?"

I darted in front of him. He still didn't understand!

"Dad, listen. The armor's not just haunted. It's dangerous. The knight tried to chop me into a million pieces. He tried to—"

I might as well have told the story to the wall.

Dad didn't hear a word I said. I had never seen him so excited.

"This is great! Better than great! The armor really is haunted. Carly. Mike." He turned to us. "You're looking at the most brilliant man on Fear Street. We'll make a mint. We'll . . ."

He went on and on like that. The more he went on, the lower my shoulders sagged.

"Did he really come down off his horse by himself, Mike?" he asked me. "Did he walk? Did he say anything?"

"Yes, he walked! Yes, he talked!" I yelled at Dad. "And then he tried to slice me in half with a huge sword!"

I never yelled at Dad. We weren't allowed. But this was an emergency.

If he would only listen for two seconds.

I snatched the sleeve of his gray robe.

"Dad, the ghost is here—now. The curse is on us. Whoever owns the armor is doomed. You've got to believe me!"

Dad laughed. He still didn't get it. Or maybe he thought I was acting so crazy because I'd seen a ghost.

His eyes glittered. He rubbed his hands together. "We can add an addition next spring. We'll have to, there will be so many customers."

"But, Dad. Dad, I—"

64

Dad slipped one arm around my shoulders. He grabbed Carly with the other one. He pressed us both into a huge hug. "We did it!" he said. "We saved the museum! Thanks to Uncle Basil, we've got our very own ghost."

Dad nudged us toward the stairs in the living room. "Well," he said, "I think that's enough excitement for one night. Or should I say one k-n-i-g-h-t?" He laughed at his own joke.

I didn't.

My heart sank. So did my hopes of making Dad listen.

He flicked off the kitchen light. He led us out of the museum. Dad and Carly headed up the steps. He kept talking a mile a minute. "The media, that's what we need. I'll call the TV stations in the morning. And the newspapers. We'll set up a grand opening. A grand unveiling of the haunted knight! This summer the tourists will be waiting in a line a mile long."

Still chuckling, I heard Dad tell Carly good night. Then I heard the sound of his bedroom door closing gently behind him.

Left alone, I kicked at the bottom step. Now what? I had to do something. But I couldn't figure out what.

It was no use.

I was too tired.

And too worried.

There was nothing to do but head back to bed.

I stood at the top of the steps when I thought I heard something. Something that didn't sound right.

I listened hard.

I heard it again. Louder this time.

The short hairs on the back of my neck stood up on end.

I recognized the sound.

The ghostly *clip-clop* of a horse's hooves.

The next day I rushed straight home after school. I dumped my backpack in the upstairs kitchen and grabbed some cookies. Then I ran into the museum, looking for Mr. Spellman.

Dad wouldn't listen to me. But I knew Mr. Spellman would.

I found him in the conservatory working on Sir Thomas. I saw the armor in one piece again stretched out flat on the floor next to the horse. Mr. Spellman was polishing the knight's broadsword.

He turned and smiled when I ran in. "Home from school already, Mike?" he said.

"Mr. Spellman, there you are. Dad wouldn't listen to me last night. But maybe you can warn him."

Mr. Spellman's bushy eyebrows shot up. "Warn him? About what?"

"The armor! It's haunted. Just like the story you told me," I gasped.

"That's what your dad said." He nodded. "He's making big plans for the grand opening next weekend."

"Oh, no!" I collapsed onto the floor. I shook my head. "I hope it's not too late," I said.

"Too late for what? What's wrong, pal?" Mr. Spellman sat down on the floor next to me. His old knees creaked.

I drew in a deep breath. Finally someone would listen to me. Everyone would be safe from Sir Thomas.

Even if it did ruin Dad's grand opening.

Sitting there on the floor, I told Mr. Spellman the whole story, start to finish. His blue eyes widened as he listened. He nodded a few times. But he didn't interrupt me once.

When I finished, Mr. Spellman didn't make fun of me, like Carly did. He didn't get all excited, like Dad did.

He just nodded his white head again. He pulled on his mustache. He was thinking really hard. After a little while he hoisted himself to his feet. He offered me a hand up.

"Mike, you should be proud of yourself," Mr.

68

Spellman said. "You fought the knight. You beat him. You broke the curse!"

"Do you really think so?" I asked. "But what if Sir Thomas comes back? What if I didn't break the curse? What if he's just waiting for the right time?"

"Hmmm." Mr. Spellman tugged on his mustache again. "I don't know, Mike. It sounds as if you put his evil spirit to rest for once and for all." Mr. Spellman glanced over at the armor. "He looks pretty harmless now, doesn't he?"

I looked at the armor, too. Last night, lit from within with Sir Thomas's ghostly red fire, it had terrified me. Right now in the sunlight the armor did seem harmless.

Maybe Mr. Spellman was right. Maybe I had defeated the knight for good.

But then I remembered Dad's big plans.

All the reporters. All the tourists.

Everyone expected a ghost.

"But what about Dad's big plans? No ghost, no grand opening."

"Yes, you've got a point there." He scratched his head. "Too bad your dad has invited every reporter in town."

"Every reporter?" I echoed.

"TV, radio, newspapers. The works." Mr. Spellman nodded. "He'll be crushed if there's no ghost." He sighed.

I sighed, too.

"Yeah, he'll be crushed," I said.

Mr. Spellman turned to me slowly. "Maybe we shouldn't tell him."

"We shouldn't?"

"Well, when you think about it, what good will it do? No one can guarantee when a ghost will show up anyway. Let the reporters come." He smiled. "The museum could use the publicity, right?"

"I guess so. That makes sense."

"Why upset your dad and ruin his plans?" Mr. Spellman continued in a low voice. He glanced at the armor again. "And who knows—Sir Thomas might return just to be on the five o'clock news."

I grinned. "That would really be something."

"Sure would." Mr. Spellman smiled back.

"I guess you're right," I said. "We won't tell Dad."

"We won't tell anyone," Mr. Spellman agreed.

I nodded. "But I'll keep an eye on Sir Thomas."

"Me, too." Mr. Spellman patted my shoulder. "Now I must get back to work. Want to help put Sir Thomas on his horse?"

I stood up and gazed over at the armor. I put my hands in my pockets.

"Uh—well, I really want to—" I stammered. "But I need to study for this huge math test."

Mr. Spellman chuckled. "Sure thing, Mike. Maybe next time."

He smiled and winked at me.

* * *

70

That night I couldn't sleep. I leaned back against my pillows and gazed into the blue pendant. And worried.

I worried that Sir Thomas *would* return. He'd charge through the museum and make confetti out of all of us.

Then I worried that the ghost was gone and Dad's grand opening would be a flop. And the thought almost made me wish the ghost would return.

I worried so much that I almost didn't hear it.

Thump. Thump.

I sat up. I listened.

Thump. Thump.

"Very funny, Carly." Grumbling, I got out of bed. "How dumb do you think I am?"

I went downstairs. The sounds grew louder. I followed them. Right back to the kitchen.

"The kitchen? Again?" I shook my head in amazement. Carly didn't have much of an imagination.

Without bothering to turn on the lights, I walked through the museum and into the kitchen.

Thump. Thump.

I heard it, louder than ever. But I didn't see Carly. Anywhere.

For a couple of seconds I stood stone still. I didn't take a breath. I didn't move a muscle.

Until somebody grabbed my arm.

71

I shrieked and jumped out of my slippers.

"Sorry, Mike."

Mr. Spellman! As soon as I saw him, I relaxed. But not for long.

Something was up.

Mr. Spellman put one finger up to his lips. "I didn't mean to scare you," he whispered. "I was working late in the mummy room when I heard the sound. What do you suppose it is?"

I shrugged. "Probably Carly. She has a rotten sense of humor."

Mr. Spellman crept over to the door of the conservatory. He peeked inside. "It sounds as if it's coming from in here. What do you say? Should we investigate?"

I swallowed hard. My tongue felt thick. My mouth felt dry.

"But, Mr. Spellman," I began, "what if—"

Mr. Spellman didn't let me finish. He gave me a reassuring smile. "Don't worry, Mike. We'll be really careful. I believe you about the haunted armor. I'm not going to take any chances. Not with a ghost as evil as Sir Thomas. Nothing will happen to you. I promise."

I'm not a chicken. But I know one thing. I never would have had the nerve to check out that noise without Mr. Spellman. I followed him into the conservatory.

The second we set foot inside the door, the thumping noise stopped.

Mr. Spellman made sure I stayed in back of him. He led us over to the exhibit.

I spotted Sir Thomas up on his horse. His head facing forward. His lance held high.

Nothing looked out of place.

"Well, I guess we're both wrong this time." Mr. Spellman didn't whisper anymore. He looked as relieved as I felt. "It wasn't the ghost after all."

Mr. Spellman turned around to leave the room. I did, too.

I took one step. Then something whizzed by my head. Close enough to skim my hair.

I saw Mr. Spellman's face turn white.

Then I heard something explode.

A long, thick arrow had slammed into one of Dad's flowerpots not ten feet away. The arrow stuck up from a pile of dirt and the jagged remains of the pot. I knew right away what kind of arrow it was.

It was an arrow from a crossbow.

A knight's crossbow.

Mr. Spellman and I turned around at the same moment.

Just in time to see Sir Thomas charge.

12

"**R**un for it!" I yelled at Mr. Spellman as I took off at top speed.

I headed for the door. I heard the horse's hooves pounding behind me. Getting louder. Coming closer. Closing the gap between us.

I darted to my right and the knight followed. I veered off to the left. He pulled hard on the horse's reins and stayed right behind me.

I glanced over my shoulder.

Mr. Spellman was beside me. And behind him was the knight.

The red fire behind Sir Thomas's visor was blinding. He held his lance high. I saw the sharp tip. Aimed right at me.

Up ahead the door seemed an impossible distance away.

I pushed myself harder. My lungs burned. I reached out desperately. The door still looked miles away.

Another second and the lance would be right through my back.

I heard a noise. A *whooshing* sound. Like rushing wind.

I braced myself for the blow.

Nothing happened.

I spun around. So scared that I grabbed Mr. Spellman's hand.

All the lances from Dad's exhibit came whizzing off the wall and over my head. Aimed right at the knight.

Some of the lances hit the floor right in front of Sir Thomas and stuck there. Some of them stuck in the floor in back of him. Lances stuck up from the floor to the knight's right. They stuck up to his left.

A cage of lances surrounded him. The knight was trapped. His horse snorted. It stomped the ground.

Sir Thomas let out a deafening roar. He waved his arms over his head. The red flames behind his visor shimmered.

"Wow!" I was flabbergasted. And relieved. I let go of Mr. Spellman. I took a chance and went over to the lances to check them out.

How did this happen? I couldn't figure it out.

That's when I noticed my pendant.

The blue smoke inside the marble swirled and bubbled. Glimmering with a weird blue light. Brighter than Sir Thomas's spooky eyes.

"Wow!" I know, I should have been able to come up with something better to say, but "Wow" seemed to cover all the bases.

It had to be the pendant. It was magic!

Now it had saved me for a second time.

What else could make a papier-mâché rock destroy a suit of armor? What else could make a row of lances fly through the air?

"That's it! That's it, Mr. Spellman. Don't you get it?" I held the pendant up to the moonlight. "You were right! The first time you saw it you knew. The pendant! It *is* magic!"

Still holding the pendant up, I stepped closer to the knight.

Mr. Spellman stood behind me. This time the swords Dad had hung on the wall for display clattered against each other. Battle-axes streaked by in the air.

Awesome!

I could hardly believe it. I tested some more. Waving the pendant, I moved toward the knight.

Sir Thomas winced. He held one metal hand up in front of his face. The red fire behind the visor flickered and faded out.

"Hear me, wicked knight. I *am* a wizard!" I tried to

make my voice low and booming. The way I thought a wizard would sound.

Loud. Important. Powerful.

"I command you to stop attacking us!"

I jabbed the pendant in Sir Thomas's direction.

The swords crashed and smashed over the knight's head. He waved his arms at them. They kept crashing and smashing.

I lifted the pendant up. The round glass orb caught the moonlight. It sparkled. Then it shot a dazzling beam of blue light at Sir Thomas.

As the light struck him, Sir Thomas sat bolt upright.

His armor shimmied and rattled for a second. And then . . .

Boom!

13

His helmet exploded off his shoulders and flew straight up to the ceiling.

A gust of red fire shot up out of the armor.

And then the whole thing fell apart.

Sir Thomas's breastplate clattered to the floor.

His shield fell out of his hands.

And then his arms fell off.

The knight's metal leg guards tottered, then hit the ground.

An awful smell, like burning rubber, hung in the air.

The knight had turned into a pile of scrap metal.

A spooky cloud of red smoke floated above the whole mess.

I held my nose and took a step closer. I heard a soft hissing. Soft, like air leaking out of a tire. I looked down at the pile of armor.

He was gone all right. Gone for good this time.

"I did it! I did it! Way to go, Conway!" I had never been so excited in my whole, entire life. I did a little dance through the last wisps of smoke.

"I really *am* a wizard!"

Then I heard another voice. A strange and chilling one.

"You witless newt! You did nothing. Nothing! I did it all!"

I froze in my tracks. This voice really did sound like a wizard. It boomed through the conservatory. The windows rattled all around me. The floor shook under my feet. The whole place filled with a swirling icy wind that made me shiver.

I spun around, looking for the source of that frightening voice.

"Fool! Do you really believe you possess magic powers?" The voice was coming from Mr. Spellman? Could it be?

He laughed and frosty fingers raced up my spine.

He smiled at me in a way I'd never seen him smile before. A way I didn't like.

His teeth looked pointy and sharp. His skin pulled tight across his face. Like a skull.

Something about his creepy smile made me feel as

79

if I'd been kicked right in the stomach. I couldn't believe it. I stepped closer to my friend. "Mr. Spellman?"

Mr. Spellman waved his hands. The motion made the air ripple all around me. My skin suddenly felt clammy. I broke out in a cold sweat.

"Do not call me by that ridiculous name, boy!" Mr. Spellman roared. "I am Mardren, the greatest wizard of all time! And now, little bug, I am finished with you!"

Slowly Mr. Spellman raised both his hands. They were covered with golden rings shaped like snakes. The snakes had glowing red and purple jewel eyes that winked in the moonlight. He pointed right at me.

The snake rings came alive. They slithered around his fingers. The snakes grew bigger and bigger. They crawled around his wrists, hissing. Ugly black tongues flickered at me.

A snake head darted out at me. I saw its jaws stretch open and long curved fangs poised to strike.

I leaped back.

Mr. Spellman waved his hands again. The hissing golden snakes transformed into lightning bolts, flashing from his fingertips. The lightning crackled in the air all around me. So close, I felt the lightning's heat as it zipped by my head.

I ducked down. Almost too late.

80

I smelled burning hair and touched my head. A few strands on top felt hot and singed.

I couldn't believe it. Mr. Spellman. My friend. All this time he tricked me. He tricked everyone!

Crouched down in a corner, I watched as his body transformed.

His eyes glowed. Not red like the knight's. White. Cold. Icy. Hard.

The skin on his face shimmered, like a bowl of Jell-O. Then it turned a sickly yellow-green color that looked dry and leathery. The lines around his eyes and mouth grew deeper and his nose stretched out, long and beak-shaped.

His mustache grew out, too. Long and wild-looking. And his cheeks sprouted a beard. A white beard, all tangled and knotted, that flowed down to his waist.

He waved one hand above his head, and suddenly a long silver stick appeared in his hand.

Then he twirled around, swinging the stick around over his head.

One. Two. Three times.

He spun at top speed, spinning into a complete blur. A purple blur.

I blinked.

He stopped and stood before me. A long purple robe flowed around his body. Purple boots covered his feet and a tall, pointed purple hat balanced on his head.

Symbols that glowed with strange light covered his robe and hat. Silver moons. Golden stars. Strange shapes I'd never seen before.

I saw a big blue circle, too. With swirling blue lights inside.

"My pendant!" I stared at the symbol on Mr. Spellman's robe. I looked down at my pendant.

It softly glowed.

"Mike, Mike, Mike." Mr. Spellman . . . er, Mardren laughed. I felt a creepy, pins-and-needles tingle all over my body. "You really thought you did it all, didn't you?" Mardren shook his head. He smiled a scary smile. "You ridiculous worm! You have no magic power. The power is all mine. I merely used you to destroy my most deadly foe."

Mardren pointed his long silver stick. Right at the pile of armor. With the toe of one purple boot he kicked aside Sir Thomas's helmet. It rolled into the corner.

Mardren chuckled. "Once every hundred years, Sir Thomas and I must fight each other," he explained. "If I defeat him, his ghost is doomed. He must stay a prisoner inside his armor for another hundred years. If he defeats me . . ." Mardren shrugged.

"Well, that is not going to happen, is it? At least not for another hundred years. You took care of that for me."

A memory flashed through my head. I thought about what the knight told me. About fighting the wizard as a dragon. And as a wall of fire.

"You are correct!" Mardren could read my mind! He said out loud everything I was thinking. "Sir Thomas thought you were me. He thought I had taken on the shape of a small, weak boy. It is not what I had planned. Not exactly. But it worked. Why do you think a wizard of my skill and power would hang around in this shabby place?"

The wizard looked around the conservatory. His face puckered up. His nostrils flared.

"With my powers I knew Sir Thomas would arrive here sooner or later. I knew it even before your uncle Basil found the armor in Dreadbury Castle and sent it here. I had to wait for Sir Thomas. I had to fight him."

Mardren stared hungrily at my pendant. His tongue flickered over his cracked lips. He smiled.

A shiver crawled up my back.

"You snatched the pendant before I could, bothersome boy," Mardren said. "That day the armor was delivered you reached first for the magic orb. You touched it first and put it on. There is a spell that gives the pendant its power. After you touched it, I could not take it away from you. No one could. Not until Sir Thomas was destroyed. Now . . ."

A slow smile inched up the edges of Mardren's mustache. He looked down at the pieces of Sir Thomas scattered on the floor. His eyes glittered.

"You took care of that for me. And I never faced any danger. If anyone had to get killed . . ." Mardren shook out his robe. The moons and stars on it flashed at me. "You see what I mean? Everything is perfect now. . . ."

Mardren swung around. He pointed his staff toward me. A single bolt of lightning flashed from the end of it. It shot right at my chest.

The pendant flashed, as if it answered the call of Mardren's magic. It rose right up off my chest. It jerked toward Mardren. It tugged me closer to the wizard.

"You have something that belongs to me, toad." Mardren touched the golden chain with the tip of his staff. The chain snapped. When Mardren lifted his staff, the blue marble globe stuck to the top of it.

"Now I have the magic pendant," Mardren said. "And Sir Thomas can no longer stop me from using it. This magic orb will make me even more powerful." He glanced at the marble. His face lit up with an evil smile.

Mardren looked down at me. "I am afraid I must get rid of you. I cannot allow you to give away my little secret. Hmmm. What should I do?"

Mardren sucked on his shriveled lower lip, thinking. Thinking about getting rid of me.

I swallowed hard. I quietly slid back a step. Run for it, I urged myself.

"Not so fast, toad!" he boomed at me. Mardren's look froze me on the spot. His eyes lit up. "That's it! I know exactly what to do. I will turn you into a mouse. Just be careful! Don't get too close to the cat!"

I caught my breath. It burned my lungs. My hands trembled at my sides.

Mardren saw me shake. Chuckling, he waved his hands over my head. "Keep still, pesky boy! The words of power must be spoken three times." He cleared his throat. His voice rang through the room.

"With the moon over the house, change this boy into a mouse. With the moon over the house, change this boy into a mouse. With the moon over the house, change this boy—"

"Stop!" another voice shouted.

Mardren gasped in surprise.

The voice sounded from the deep shadows on the other side of the conservatory. A deep hollow voice. It echoed. It rumbled.

My heart thumping, I watched a shape materialize out of the shadows. Slowly it clomped forward. With each step I could see more of it.

Metal shoes.

A broad breastplate.

A helmet with an empty space behind the visor.

The knight raised one metal glove. He pointed right at Mardren. His voice boomed.

"Wizard! You will not win!"

14

Sir Thomas. Back again!

The knight lumbered out of the shadows. He took one shaky step forward. Then another.

I stared at the knight—and gasped.

It wasn't Sir Thomas.

One of dad's fake suits of armor had come alive!

"Wh-what's going on here?" I stuttered. Was the ghost of Sir Thomas in *there* now?

I stepped back as the knight clattered forward—his sights set on Mardren this time.

I shot a glance at Mardren. Then the knight. Which one should I run from? Which one?

Before I could move, the wizard's eyes flashed. He

shook his shoulders. He spread his arms. He started the words of another spell.

The knight stomped closer. He swung out at the wizard with his long metal arm.

He missed Mardren by a mile. But one of his heavy metal gloves smacked the pendant on top of Mardren's staff.

The big blue marble wobbled. It teetered. It tumbled from the top of the staff.

Mardren lunged for it, grabbing for the beautiful blue marble as it fell through the air.

The tips of his long, gnarled fingers brushed it.

It slipped past his fingers.

And crashed to the floor.

The glass shattered, and a deafening boom echoed through the room. Louder than a clap of thunder.

A brilliant blue light flashed—flashed so bright I had to cover my eyes.

Then I heard a strange fizzing sound.

The pendant had burst into a zillion pieces. And now some of the shards of glass zipped through the air. Zipped through the air like tiny shooting stars!

Then a cloud of blue smoke swirled up from the floor. Up from the center of the jagged bits of glass that remained there.

It was the most amazing thing I had ever seen.

The blue mist floated over the floor like the fog that

88

sometimes hovers over the Fear Street Cemetery. It curled around my legs. Everywhere it touched me I felt cold to the bone.

Then it gathered in a cloud around Mardren. It slowly rose up, up, up over his flowing robe.

"No! No!" Mardren screamed. He waved his arms frantically. Trying to wave away the smoke. But the smoke continued to billow.

He puffed up his cheeks and blew at it.

Then he kicked at it with his purple boots.

The blue smoke thinned—and Mardren fell to his knees. Searching. Searching the floor for something.

What? What is he looking for? I wondered, staring hard through the mist.

And that's when I saw it.

A tiny golden sword—glittering in the moonlight.

I blinked in amazement. It must have been hidden in the marble the whole time. Hidden by the swirling smoke.

Mardren grabbed for the sword at the same time I did.

I reached it first.

"Slow as a snail!" I cried.

I snatched up the sword. The moment my fingertips touched it, a jolt of electricity shot through my hand. Raced up my arm. Hit me square in the chest, hard. I staggered back.

My fingers tingled—as if hundreds of pins and needles were piercing them. I didn't care. I held the tiny sword tight in my fist.

Another jolt shot through my hand.

Sparks flew from my fist.

I gaped at my hand—as the tiny sword began to grow, right in the center of my palm.

It grew and grew. Longer. Thicker. Heavier.

It grew until it was the size of a real knight's sword.

I grabbed on to its handle. It fit perfectly in my grip.

I stretched out my arm and waved it. The blade caught the moonlight. It twinkled with the light of a hundred stars.

Then a *whooshing* sound rushed through my ears. And, out of nowhere, pieces of golden armor appeared in the air. Like magic, they snapped onto my body.

Golden shin guards clicked onto my knees to protect my legs. A golden breastplate snapped over my chest.

Golden gloves slipped over my hands. And golden metal sleeves sprang out from them, covering my arms.

"All right!" I whooped.

My voice sounded funny. Echoing inside the helmet that had suddenly appeared over my head.

Holding the golden sword high, I spun around and faced Mardren.

I thought the wizard looked mad before. But that must have been his "have a nice day" face.

Mardren tossed back his head. His lips curled into a sneer—revealing his long, pointed teeth. He let out an ugly snarl. Sparks of lightning crackled from his fingertips.

"So you think you can defeat me?" he howled. A heavy wind whipped through the room, nearly knocking me down. "Nothing can destroy my magic!" he roared.

Mardren spread his arms wide—and started to grow. Into a towering giant.

A huge bolt of lightning exploded from the tip of his staff.

The conservatory lit up with a blinding white light. It hurt my eyes, and I squeezed them shut.

The lightning bolt hung in the air. It sizzled. Cracked and snapped. I could feel its intense heat through my armor—the heavy golden metal singed my skin.

With a sweep of his arm Mardren sent the deadly hot bolt on its course.

On its course—straight at me.

15

I leaped in the air. Just in time.

The lightning streaked beneath me. Inches below my metal shoes.

I staggered back and landed in the arms of the knight.

"Don't give up, Mike." The knight whispered the words against my helmet.

"Carly?" I gasped. "Is that you, Carly?"

"Yes!" she whispered, peeking out of the space between the breastplate and the bottom of the helmet. All I could see were her beady little eyes.

"You distract him," I whispered. "I'll run up and take my best shot."

"I can't see what I'm doing in this soup can," she

said. She pushed me back on my feet. "You've got to fight him alone!"

Then she shoved me forward.

I shook from head to toe. My armor rattled. I lifted one heavy leg and raised my sword.

Mardren stood tall. He sneered a wicked sneer.

I stared into his eyes, about to strike.

Mardren stretched out his arms. He held up a silver stick and waved his arms. His purple robe billowed all around him.

I jumped back.

He tossed his head back and shrieked long and loud. The skin on his face shimmered again, stretching out in all directions. His arms stretched out, his hands turning into big scaly yellow claws. His legs stretched, too, and his body puffed up, like a huge purple blimp.

Cackling wickedly, he floated up from the floor and sailed above me.

I staggered back. My mouth hung open.

I saw his neck stretch out and his beaky nose grow into a long snout. He swooped up to the very top of the ceiling, spinning around in the shadows.

I held tightly to my sword, getting ready for . . . I didn't know what!

I squinted at his dark, twisting form, sailing above me. Then it swooped down. Coming in for a landing.

I crouched down and covered my head.

Flapping wings beat the air and something huge snarled and hissed.

I gulped and looked up again.

I stood face-to-face with a dragon.

A gigantic, hideous dragon with big purple wings.

All over its huge body purple scales oozed foul-smelling slime. Three big yellow eyes rolled around in its head. Two long black forked tongues curled out its mouth. Disgusting green saliva dripped everywhere. The gluey drops sizzled as they hit the floor. The tiles vaporized.

I took a step forward. I swung my sword with both hands wrapped around the handle.

The dragon twisted its ugly head back. The two tongues curled out at me. The dragon sucked in a deep breath. Then blew it out. A putrid cloud hit me. It smelled horrible.

The disgusting stink turned my stomach upside down. It burned my eyes. Inside my armor I gasped for air.

I saw the dragon's huge jaws gape open again. I jumped back and braced myself for the smell.

My eyes widened as I saw a long stream of fire spew out his mouth. The flames licked the toes of my armor boots. My feet were burning up.

"Hey!" I yelped. I hopped from foot to foot. The dragon drew in another deep breath. I readied myself for another huge flame.

"Oh, no, you don't!" I saw Carly running toward us with a fire extinguisher. Dad kept them all over the museum, just in case.

Carly had removed Dad's armor, and she moved just fast enough.

She leaned back and aimed at the dragon. She pulled the lever and fired.

With a *pop* and a *whoosh*, foamy white stuff flew all over the place. The plume of foam shot right down the dragon's throat. It cooled off my feet.

"Way to go, Carly!" I gave her a high five.

When I looked back at the dragon, I saw only Mardren again.

Foamy white gunk dripped off his beard. Globs of it clung to his hat and his purple robe.

His yellow face twisted with anger.

"I am through playing games!" Mardren tossed his staff up in the air. He snapped his fingers. The staff came down again and magically turned into a gleaming sword.

Mardren grabbed the sword. He charged.

"Mike, look out!" Carly screamed.

I pushed her out of the way and raised my sword.

I looked up and there was Mardren.

A sword's length away.

Mardren swung. I blocked his swing with my golden sword. The two blades crashed together.

Sparks flew everywhere. My arm vibrated. It felt as if it had been yanked right off my shoulder.

The next time Mardren came at me, I dodged his sword.

Mardren jabbed low. I jumped. As fast and as high as I could.

By the time Mardren backed off, he was breathing hard. I panted, too. We glared at each other. Beads of sweat ran down my face. Dripping into my eyes. My heart pounded against the suit of magical armor.

Struggling to catch my breath, I kept my eyes on the wizard.

He raised his sword. I saw his lips flicker. I heard him mumble.

Mumble another wicked magic spell.

Mardren raised his sword straight up toward the sky. Purple sparks burst out of the end of it.

The purple fire hit the glass ceiling. It rained down all around us. Just looking at it made me feel dizzy. And sleepy.

Not a good sign.

"Don't look at it. Don't look at it." I kept repeating the warning over and over inside my head.

But I couldn't help it.

Mardren's magic sparks glittered like jewels. The sparks hypnotized me.

"Don't fall asleep now!" I told myself. "You'll be finished!"

I kept blinking my eyes. My eyelids felt so heavy. They drooped, almost closed. I shook my head. My head felt heavy, too. Too heavy to hold up.

I felt my eyes close and my head drop against my chest.

My knees were weak. I staggered forward. My knees buckled.

"No, Mike! No!" Carly shouted at me. Her voice sounded as if it came from really far away. "Don't let him do it!"

I'm not sure how I did it, but I forced my eyes open. The purple sparks fell all around me. I didn't want to think about what would happen if they hit me.

With every last little bit of energy I had, I clasped the sword in two hands and raised my arms.

I propped my sword up on my shoulder. When the sparks got close enough, I batted them with the sword.

Line drives. Grounders. High flies to center field.

Some of the sparks sputtered and sizzled. Some of them bounced. They hit the ceiling and fell down again.

Right on top of Mardren.

"No!" the wizard shrieked. He gave a bloodcurdling scream.

The sparks hit his hat. I heard hissing. Each time one landed on him, I saw a puff of purple smoke rise. The sparks covered his purple robe. They landed all

97

around him on the floor and burst into puffs of purple smoke.

The smoke got thicker. Darker. He tried to move away, but the smoky cloud clung to him. He couldn't shake it off.

In seconds he was standing in a thick, billowing purple cloud.

"No! No! You monstrous children! How could you do this to me?" Mardren waved his arms in the smoke.

Carly crept up beside me. Side by side, we watched the purple cloud cover Mardren from head to toe. And then close in on him.

"No! No!" Mardren's eyes bulged. His mouth twisted in a gruesome scowl.

I could hardly see him anymore. The weird symbols on his robe were dissolving in the smoke. Then his long white beard went up in smoke.

The smoke spread over his face. The cloud covered his eyes. The last thing to disappear was the very tip of the wizard's purple, pointy hat.

"No! No! No!" From out of the smoky cloud we heard Mardren's smothered voice. He whined and groaned. "This can't be happening. Not to me. You evil children! I am Mardren, the most powerful wizard in all the world. No! No . . ."

Mardren's voice got weaker and weaker. Finally I couldn't hear it anymore. The huge cloud of purple smoke swirled around. An awful smell made me choke and cough.

Except for my coughing, the place was suddenly as quiet as a tomb.

Carly and I stood there, listening. Waiting to see what would happen next.

From out of nowhere a cold wind swept through the conservatory. The purple cloud blew away.

Mardren had vanished completely in the smoke.

Or had he?

Right at the spot where the wizard had vanished, I saw something. A huge, hideous purple snail.

"Yuck!" Carly jerked back.

"He can't hurt us anymore." I went a little bit closer to the snail. Bulging red eyes dangled from the ends of long yellow antennae. Thick slime covered a big purple shell. A slimy snail body, a disgusting shade of green, wriggled beneath the shell.

I poked the snail with my golden sword. "Slow as a snail!" I said.

The snail's antennae wiggled in the air, and its eyes bugged out. It tossed its disgusting head. Then it slithered away.

All that was left of Mardren was a trail of purple slime.

16

"Mike, you were . . . you were . . ." Carly shook her head. Her smile grew wider and wider. "You were awesome!"

I whipped off my helmet. I couldn't help myself. I smiled, too.

"I *was* awesome, wasn't I?" I waved my sword over my head. I laughed.

"You were pretty awesome, too, Carly," I admitted. "What made you put on that armor?"

"I was going to play a joke on you," she admitted. "But then I heard what Mr. Spellman . . . er . . . Mardren . . . er . . . whoever he was . . . said! I knew Dad was out. I had no choice. There was no way I'd let him turn you into a mouse. I mean, what if the cat ate you? The poor thing would have gotten sick!"

"Thanks a lot!" I was too tired to think of anything funny to say. I'd get her later. After a few hours of sleep.

I yawned and tossed my sword down. The second I did, the rest of the golden armor unsnapped. The pieces clattered to the floor.

I sighed and wiggled my shoulders. I hadn't realized how heavy the armor felt.

"Boy, it's not easy being a knight in shining armor!"

I plunked down on the floor. Right next to the charred pile of Sir Thomas's armor. Now Dad would have to put it all back together again. I poked one of Sir Thomas's shoes with the tip of my sword. I pushed aside one of his gloves.

I set the golden sword down on the floor, between me and the pile of Sir Thomas's armor.

"I feel like I ran a couple miles," I said with a huge yawn. "I can't believe I—"

Something moved next to me. My words stuck in my throat. I heard Carly's muffled scream, but I didn't dare turn to look at her.

My gaze was stuck on Sir Thomas's glove.

All by itself the glove slid out of the pile and right over to the sword. One by one the metal fingers flexed. They closed around the handle of the golden sword.

"Yikes!" I rolled out of the way. I scrambled to my feet.

With the glove still holding on tight, the sword rose in the air. I heard a deep moan. The sound raised the hairs on the back of my neck. The moan started low. And sounded far away. But it got louder by the second. And closer.

Then it surrounded us.

The sword pointed toward the pieces of armor that protected Sir Thomas's legs. With a *whoosh* they rose up off the floor. They floated over to the sword and the glove. They stopped in the place where the knight's legs would be. Next, the sword pointed to the knight's metal boots.

"Mike!" Carly's fingers dug into my arm. "Mike, do something! He's coming back to get us!"

He was! I had to do something. Fast.

I made a diving grab for the boots.

The second my fingers touched the metal, I yelped and pulled them back. The armor stung my fingertips with cold.

I rubbed my hands to warm them. I saw the boots clatter away. Clanking against the tile floor, they marched into place right under the leg guards.

The moaning grew louder. It made my ears hurt. The breastplate flew into the air. It floated into place right above the knight's legs.

The arms came after that. With a clang they

snapped into place where the breastplate met the shoulders.

The other glove flew onto the arm that didn't have a hand. That hand gripped the golden sword, too.

I felt petrified. Worse than petrified. I could feel my pulse pounding against my temples. Hammering so hard, I felt my head about to explode.

Carly and I stared at Sir Thomas.

He stood before us in one piece again.

All except for his head.

With a piercing whistle that made the hair on my arms stand up on end, the sword swung and pointed at Sir Thomas's helmet.

With an answering wail that came from inside, the helmet slowly rose off the floor.

The helmet sailed past us. The air turned icy as it flew by.

The helmet glided over to the rest of the armor. With a click, it floated down into place.

The second it did, the fire behind the visor flared to life.

Sir Thomas's eyes flashed. They sparked. Not purple like Mardren's magical sparks.

Red.

Bloodred.

Sir Thomas didn't say a word. He lifted his sword. He pressed the tip of it against my heart.

17

Sliced to ribbons.

We were about to be sliced to ribbons.

I watched the ugly fire in Sir Thomas's eyes flicker. He stepped forward and I felt the knife point jab me through my T-shirt.

I held my breath and waited to feel his sword run me through.

The knight turned his head. He looked at the puddle of smelly purple slime. Then he turned back and looked at me.

"Who has destroyed Mardren?" His question echoed from inside the armor.

I tried to answer him. But all that came out was a sputtering, choking sound.

Carly pushed me forward. "Mike did it," she said. "He turned the wizard's own magic against him."

The knight didn't move. I could feel his gaze burning from behind the visor.

"Is this true?" he asked.

"Yes," I croaked. "I didn't have much choice. First he tried to turn me into a mouse and then he shot purple sparks at me. But I batted them back at him. With that."

I pointed at the golden sword. My hand shook like crazy. "When the sparks hit Mardren, he was smothered in a cloud of purple smoke. Then he turned into a snail. A big, slimy purple one."

"A snail!" Sir Thomas boomed with laughter. His laugh had a deep metallic ring that echoed through the room. "A slimy purple snail! How fitting for the evil one!"

He laughed and laughed, and the red fire behind the visor settled down to a warm glow.

Suddenly he didn't seem nearly as scary. He didn't seem scary at all.

Sir Thomas knelt on one knee. He bowed his head. "Then, good sir, I owe you my thanks."

"What?" I looked down at his shining helmet. He still held his sword, but now it rested on the floor. "Is this some kind of trick? You mean you've stopped trying to chop me into little pieces?"

Sir Thomas shook his head. "You must forgive

105

me," he said. "When I saw you with the pendant, I thought you were Mardren. I thought the evil wizard had changed himself into a boy to deceive me. I see now that I was wrong. You were not in league with the wicked sorcerer." The knight looked around the museum. "All of you here, you were never my enemies. You were always my friends."

"Me?" I pointed at myself. A big, goofy smile lit up my face. "I'm your friend?"

"That is correct." Sir Thomas struggled to stand up. In spite of all the oil Dad had used on him, his joints were still pretty rusty. He creaked and wobbled.

I offered him a hand.

This time when I touched the metal, it didn't chill me to the bone.

"I know the story Mardren must have told you," the knight said once he came to his feet. "He told you I was evil. Am I right?"

I nodded.

"Mardren was a scoundrel. A vile and hateful creature." Sir Thomas raised his head. He held it high. "I was never evil. Mardren was the evil one. Many hundreds of years ago I fell in love with his beautiful daughter. He would not allow us to marry. He wanted her to have a husband who was richer and more powerful than I. He put a spell on me, trapping me forever in my suit of armor. I could only be free if

Mardren was defeated. And only one thing could defeat him—my golden sword."

Sir Thomas went over to the purple puddle. He touched it with the toe of his boot.

"But Mardren imprisoned my sword inside his magic pendant," he said. "Even though the pendant remained with me, I couldn't use it. I could never retrieve the sword inside. Without its power I grew weaker and weaker. I knew I'd never be able to fight the wizard. But you did it for me, Mike."

Sir Thomas laughed again. The sound made me feel warm. The way you feel laughing with a friend. "Because of your bravery, I will finally be free of this armor, which has been my prison and my tomb. But first . . ."

Sir Thomas poked his sword in my direction. He waved me closer. "Come here, boy. And kneel."

"I don't know, Mike. . . ." Carly grabbed for my sleeve. I knew she still wasn't sure I could trust him.

But I did trust him. I had a feeling I knew exactly what Sir Thomas wanted to do.

My chest swelled with pride. I went over to the knight. I knelt in front of him.

Sir Thomas raised the sword. He brought it down again, first on my right shoulder. Then on my left. "I, Sir Thomas Barlayne, do dub thee, Sir Michael of the . . . of the . . ." Sir Thomas struggled for the right title.

"How about Sir Michael of History's Mysteries?" I suggested.

"Well said!" Sir Thomas chuckled. "I do dub thee Sir Michael of History's Mysteries."

Sir Thomas stepped back. He held his sword in front of him with both hands. He glanced at Carly. He looked at me. "I will always remember you, my friends," he said. "Now I can rest."

A blue fog rose all around Sir Thomas. It wasn't anything like the purple smoke that smothered Mardren. This was a soft cloud. It hugged Sir Thomas like a favorite blanket. I heard him sigh.

When the cloud blew away, Sir Thomas was gone.

18

"**S**o that's the story. I'm really sorry, Dad. I know how much you wanted a haunted suit of armor. I didn't mean to get rid of the ghost. It just sort of worked out that way."

"That's okay, Mike." Dad ruffled my hair. "I understand what happened. You sure were brave."

Dad put one arm around my shoulders. Carly was standing not too far away. He grabbed her, too. "You, too," he added, laughing. "And just think, all that time we had a wizard in the museum and we didn't even know it."

Carly shivered. "He wasn't a very nice wizard."

"That's for sure." I wanted to shiver, too. But I figured Sir Michael of History's Mysteries would never shiver in public.

Dad grinned. "Wait until I tell Uncle Basil. He's the one who started all this. If he didn't buy Sir Thomas's suit of armor—"

"Mr. Conway!" Someone rapped on the front door and called inside. "Mr. Conway, it's Stanley. From Stanley's Moving and Storage."

Stanley sounded as nervous today as he had the last time he came.

I glanced at Dad. Dad glanced at Carly. Carly stared at me. We all shrugged. Then we raced to the front porch.

When we reached the porch, we all screeched to a stop.

"What is it?" I looked at the huge, wooden crate that Stanley and his helper were lifting out of the van. It had red stamps all over it that said FRAGILE. Stanley and the other guy carried the crate up the front steps. They set it down on the porch. "Who's it from?"

"I don't know." Dad thanked the moving guys. They got back into their van as fast as they could. They were already halfway down Fear Street by the time Dad took out his crowbar.

He worked on the lid, loosening the nails and pushing it up.

Together, we lifted the cover off the crate. The whole box was packed with shredded paper.

"I don't know. . . ." Carly bit her lip. "I don't think

I like the looks of this. I'm sure not sticking my hand in there again."

"I don't like the looks of this, either." Dad took a deep breath. "Well, here goes," he said, and stuck his arm into the paper.

I held my breath.

I wondered what we'd see when Dad pulled his arm out again.

Would it be a helmet with fiery eyes peering out from it? Or a magical pendant filled with blue smoke? Or maybe that yucky purple snail, all slimy and smelly?

Dad pulled his hand out. He held a long white envelope.

"What's this?" He frowned and stared at it. "Should we open it?" he asked us.

But before Carly and I could answer, he tore the envelope open. He pulled out a letter and unfolded it. "Looks like a note from your uncle Basil," he said.

"It is?" Carly and I darted forward at the same time. I got to the letter first.

I snatched the letter out of Dad's hands.

"What does it say?" Carly asked.

I looked down at the letter. I cleared my throat. "It says: 'Dear Barnaby, Mike, and Carly. Well, here it is. The armor I promised you. Sorry it took so long to get to you. I don't know if the legend is true, but the old guy who sold it to me says the armor is haunted. I hope so, don't you? See you when I get back.'"

I blinked in surprise. "Does this mean what I think this means?"

"It means . . ." Dad made a face. His glasses jumped up his nose. "I think it means that wherever Sir Thomas's suit of armor came from, it sure didn't come from Uncle Basil."

"Wow!" I flopped down on the edge of the crate.

"Yeah." Dad said. "Wow!"

"Wait, there's more!" Carly pointed at the letter. "There's a P.S. 'Mike, there's something extra special for you in the crate.'"

All the color drained out of Carly's face. "Not another magic pendant!"

We all reached into the crate together. We felt around in the paper.

I found the package first. It was soft. It was wrapped in brown paper.

My heart thumping, I tore off the paper. Some sort of white material. A T-shirt.

I shook it out—and read what it said.

"My uncle went to England, and all I got was this dumb shirt."

THE OOZE

R.L. STINE'S

GHOSTS OF
FEAR STREET

THE OOZE

THE OOZE

Most kids don't have to beg their dogs to chase a ball. But Tubby isn't like most dogs.

"Get the ball, Tubby!" I pleaded as I wound up for the throw. "You can do it!"

Tubby wagged his tail. Then he noticed it moving and tried to bite it.

"Come on, Tubby!" I shouted. I hurled the yellow tennis ball. It flew right by his face.

Tubby plopped down on the grass. He didn't even blink as the ball whizzed by.

The sliding back door slammed. I turned and saw my older sister, Michelle, walking toward me. As usual, she had a textbook tucked under her arm.

"When are you going to face reality, Al?" she asked

as she sat down under the apple tree. "Your dog is a total moron!"

"No, he isn't," I protested. "He just doesn't feel like playing now. Right, Tubby?" I dropped down next to him and patted his big head. His shaggy brown and white fur felt warm from the sun.

Michelle snorted and opened her calculus textbook.

"You're studying?" I asked. "On a Saturday? And you call Tubby stupid?"

"I want to graduate with the highest grades in my whole ninth-grade class," Michelle said.

Michelle is fourteen, just three years older than I am. But she's already doing college-level math.

If you haven't figured it out already, being smart means everything to her. And to my parents, too. The three of them are genuises. I mean it. They are really genuises.

It's a pain. Teachers are always asking me if I'm Michelle Sterner's little brother. When I say yes, they expect me to study twenty-four hours a day. The way she does.

I'm smart. Probably as smart as Michelle. But I don't want to spend my whole life with my nose in a book. I like to have fun.

All Michelle likes to do is study, study, study. If you ask me, she's too smart for her own good.

Tubby rose slowly to his feet with a big sigh. He wandered over to the hedge that runs along the side of the yard and began to dig.

Then he trotted over to Michelle and started a new hole there.

A few minutes later he had another hole going by the back fence.

Michelle shook her head. "Your dog is so stupid he can't even remember where he buried his bone. You should get a cat," Michelle told me. "Cats are very intelligent."

"Like Chester?" I asked. Chester is Michelle's cat. Michelle thinks he is *brilliant.*

"Did I tell you he can count up to eight now?" Michelle asked.

"Can he multiply and divide, too?" I joked.

Michelle stuck her tongue out at me. "He can snap up the window shade when he wants some light. And he knows how to jump on the electric can opener when he's hungry. And—"

"Who cares if he's smart?" I interrupted. "That's not what pets are for."

But Michelle paid no attention to me. "I saw a cat on TV that learned how to flush the toilet," she continued. "I'm teaching Chester how to do it, too."

"Boy, are you lazy, Michelle. Why can't you flush the toilet yourself?"

"He won't be flushing it for me, you jerk. I'm going to teach him how to use the bathroom—the way we do. And then we won't need kitty litter anymore!"

"Michelle, you're losing it. You're totally losing it."

"You're just jealous because you can't even teach

Tubby to fetch. Face it, Al. Chester is a billion times smarter than your dog. He's probably even smarter than you."

"You're a riot, Michelle. A real riot."

"If you ask Chester nicely," Michelle went on, "I'm sure he'll teach you how to flush the toilet, too!"

"Let's go inside, Tubby," I called out to my dog. "We don't need to listen to this!"

I crossed the lawn and grabbed Tubby's collar. I had to tug on it three times—hard—before he figured out I wanted him to come with me. Then we went inside.

Mom stood at the kitchen counter, icing a cake. "Don't look, Al!" she said, waving a spatula with chocolate all over it.

Little flecks of chocolate dotted Mom's face. They looked like extra-big freckles. Mom and I both have a ton of freckles, and the same red hair and brown eyes.

"But, Mom!" I exclaimed. "Today's my birthday. I already know that's my birthday cake." You don't have to be a genius to figure this one out, I thought.

"I still want it to be a surprise," she said firmly. "Go wait in your room. And don't come out until you hear us singing. You can work on memorizing all the capitals of South American countries for school."

I sighed. "I know every single one of them by heart, Mom."

"How about studying for Wednesday's Science Bowl?" Mom suggested.

4

I shrugged and headed down the hall to my room, dragging Tubby behind me. Around my house, if you aren't studying for one thing, you're studying for another.

Mom and Dad are research scientists. Which is how I came to be named Al, after Albert Einstein himself.

I guess I can't blame them for hoping I'd turn out to be some kind of scientific genius. But I wish they could understand that playing baseball and hanging out with my friends isn't a waste of my "wonderful brain," as my mom says.

Tubby yawned and collapsed on the floor the moment we hit my room. I reached for my copy of *Super Blades* magazine and dropped down on my bed.

I wondered what Mom and Dad had planned for my birthday this year. They always take Michelle and me to something cultural on our birthdays. Sometimes it's a concert, or if I'm really out of luck, we go to an opera.

They always give us presents that are educational, too. Boring. Totally boring.

I wanted this year to be different. So I hinted for a pair of in-line skates. And I was pretty obvious about it. I left the ads for my favorites all over the place.

Plus, I never missed a chance to mention them—making them sound real educational. I told my mom that in-line skates were excellent for eye-motor co-ordination.

I told Michelle that they improved your split-second decision-making process.

I told my dad about the big skate sale at Dalby's.

I hoped they figured it out. For three *brilliant* people, they can be pretty dense sometimes.

As I flipped through *Super Blades,* I heard footsteps stomping down the basement stairs. That meant they were almost ready to start singing. We always use the basement for celebrations.

I dropped my skating magazine on the floor and jumped off the bed. "Ready?" I yelled down the hall.

"Almost, Al!" my father called.

I was really excited. I could almost feel those in-line skates on my feet!

"Say when!" I shouted.

I couldn't stand the suspense one more second.

"Now?" I yelled.

"Now!"

I broke into a run.

I jerked open the basement door and saw Mom and Dad at the bottom of the stairs. Michelle stood in front of them, holding the cake. All the candles were lit.

They started to sing "Happy Birthday."

I walked down the steps slowly, gazing around the basement, trying to spot my present.

My eyes darted to Mom's computer station.

Nothing there.

I glanced at the big table in the middle of the room.

6

It had one of Michelle's experiments on top. That's all.

Then I glimpsed the solar motorboat my dad was working on. Thousands of high-tech tools surrounded it. No present.

Nothing.

I don't believe this, I thought. I'm not getting skates—I'm not getting a birthday present at all.

I had three more steps to go. I shot one last look around, but I didn't see anything with wrapping paper on it.

I finally reached the bottom of the stairs, right where Michelle and my parents stood—and got the biggest surprise of my life.

2

BOOM!

A huge explosion rocked the basement.

The floor, the walls—everything shook. Michelle's experiment soared from the table and crashed to the floor. Dad's tools flew everywhere.

I screamed as the force of the blast knocked me down. I landed with a thud on the hard cement.

Mom, Dad, and Michelle hovered over me. Laughing. Laughing their heads off.

"You aren't hurt, are you, Al?" Mom asked, still chuckling.

"I'm okay," I grumbled. "What's going on? What's so funny?"

"Surprise!" Dad sang out. "We wanted to celebrate your birthday with a big bang!"

"Uh, great," I said, brushing myself off.

"He doesn't get it," Michelle announced.

"Get what?" I hated to admit it, but I really was confused.

"We're giving you a chemistry set!" Mom explained. She stepped aside. Behind her, on the floor, sat a huge box—with the words *Future Scientist* printed in big red letters across the front.

"Welcome to the wonderful world of chemistry, Al," Dad said. "You're going to have all sorts of exciting adventures with this set!"

He glanced down at the broken glass and spilled chemicals on the floor. "Michelle had to borrow a few things from your set to make the bang. Don't worry. We'll replace everything."

"Thanks a lot, Mom. Dad," I mumbled. "The chemistry set is so . . ."

"So stimulating?" Dad asked.

"That's exactly the word I was looking for," I said.

"Do you *really* like it, Al?" Mom asked.

"I love it, Mom," I lied.

I didn't want to hurt their feelings. I could see that they thought the chemistry set was an incredible present.

I told you they could be dense.

Trying hard to hide my disappointment, I opened

the box and checked out the rack of test tubes inside. But when I picked up a tube with green liquid inside, Dad grabbed it from me.

"Not yet, Al," he said, placing the tube back in the rack.

"Why not?" I asked.

"You need a lesson in how to handle all these chemicals," Mom said.

"Remember, this isn't a toy," Dad added. "Michelle will teach you how to use the chemistry set safely."

"Why not you or Mom?" I asked.

"Oh, it's been a long time since your mother or I handled a chemistry set," Dad replied. "And Michelle's more up on things than we ever were."

"It was Michelle who made the bang," Mom added. "It was her way of saying happy birthday."

Somehow that didn't surprise me.

"Just tell Michelle when you want to start using it," Mom went on.

"I can't wait," I answered, hoping I sounded as though I meant it. "I really can't wait."

If I had known I was about to enter the worst nightmare you could imagine, I would never have opened that box.

I would have waited forever!

3

What a birthday.

First a chemistry set. Then a night at the opera—that I thought would never end.

Even when the villain finally stabbed the hero through the heart, the guy kept on singing and singing.

And today—the day after my birthday—wasn't turning out much better.

It was Sunday. To me, that meant I should be outside doing something fun. To Mom and Dad, it meant studying. So that's what I was doing—memorizing facts from my *Science Teasers* book for the Science Bowl.

Shadyside Middle School has won the state championship three years in a row. With Michelle on the team, how could they lose?

But last year Michelle went on to Shadyside High. Now everyone says it's my turn to keep up the school's winning tradition! Which is why I'm stuck in my room, studying away.

I read the first question—what is the end product of photosynthesis?

Before I could come up with the answer, I smelled something unbelievably putrid in the house. I had to investigate. People died from smells that bad!

I checked all the bedrooms as I made my way down the hall. They were empty.

As soon as I spotted Michelle in the kitchen, I knew I had found the source of the foul odor.

"You're baking brownies again, aren't you?" I accused her. "Admit it, Michelle!"

"Don't touch them!" she snarled, stepping in front of the counter, blocking them from view. "Don't even look at them!"

"Too late," I told her. "I already saw them. They're burnt to a crisp!"

"They're just a little brown around the edges," she declared. "My chess club will love them."

"You're going to poison your friends?" I asked. "Even for you, that's low."

Someone knocked at the door, and Michelle sprang

12

for it. But I got there first. Colin, my best friend, stepped inside.

"Oh, it's just you," Michelle muttered.

"Whoa!" Colin said. "What's wrong with *just me?*"

"Her chess club is having a meeting here," I explained. "She was probably hoping you were Jonathan Muller. He's the president of the club, and she has a total crush on him."

"I do not!" Michelle snapped. But her face turned bright red.

"Yeah, right," I answered. "You should see her looseleaf binder." I grinned at Colin. "She has entire pages with 'Michelle Sterner-Muller' written all over them. She wants to marry the guy or something."

Colin snickered. Michelle threw a potholder at me. "What were you doing snooping in my binder?" she shrieked. "That's my personal property!"

I threw the potholder back at her. "Mom said I could," I informed her, "because I ran out of looseleaf paper."

Michelle glared at me. "If you tell anyone, I'll kill you." She turned to Colin. "You, too," she threatened.

"It's cool," Colin said. "Can I have a brownie?"

Before I could stop him, Colin popped a killer brownie into his mouth.

"Excuse me while I dial the paramedics," I said.

"Hey, they're unbelievable!" Colin exclaimed.

"See?" Michelle replied proudly.

"They are totally unbelievable." Colin swallowed. "How do you get them to taste like charcoal?"

I gave Colin a high five. "Score!" he yelled. "Two points!"

"Get out of here, you idiots!" Michelle screamed.

"Come on, Colin," I said. "Let's go down to the basement. I want to show you my birthday present."

"Oh, yeah! I can't wait to see the skates," Colin answered.

I shook my head. "Didn't get them."

"No way!" Colin exclaimed. "Your parents did it to you again?"

"Yep." What else was there to say?

I led Colin downstairs. Chester, Michelle's *brilliant* cat, followed us. He curled up in a corner and watched as we opened the chemistry set. Watched with a look that seemed to say "I'm telling Michelle. I'm telling Michelle. You're not supposed to touch that without Michelle."

It's a good thing my sister hasn't taught him to talk yet, I thought.

Colin pulled out a test tube filled with purple crystals. "What are you supposed to do with all this stuff?"

"I don't know yet. I'm not supposed to use it until Michelle shows me how," I answered.

I heard the doorbell ring. Michelle's chess geeks were here.

"We don't have to wait for her." Colin grinned.

14

"Let's have some fun with it on our own." He reached for a test tube filled with red liquid and emptied it into a beaker.

"Better not," I warned him. "You can get into real trouble if you don't know what you're doing."

"I'm not planning anything major," Colin said. "Just a little stink bomb."

"I don't know," I said. "My mom and dad told me not—"

"We can set it off upstairs," Colin interrupted. "Don't you want to see your sister choking and gagging—right in front of that guy she likes?"

That *would* be pretty funny. At least until my parents found out.

"Where's the manual?" Colin asked, digging through the box.

"I thought you knew how to make one!" I replied.

"No. No, I don't," Colin admitted. "But the instructions must be in here somewhere.

"Oh, sure," I said sarcastically. "Just look under *S* for *stink.*"

Colin found the instruction booklet and flipped through it, shaking his head. "Nothing here," he muttered.

"Come on," I said. "Let's go out. We can go to the mall or something."

"No. Let's stay here. We don't need instructions. It can't be *that* hard to make a bad smell," Colin declared. "Your sister does it without even trying."

I laughed. Colin can always make me laugh. That's one of the reasons we're best friends.

Colin tipped the test tube of purple crystals over the red liquid.

"Colin. Don't do it," I warned.

He ignored me.

He tipped the test tube some more.

"Colin! You don't know what you're doing!" I yelled.

The purple crystals began to tumble out.

I looked at the labels on the test tubes. "Not the red and the purple, Colin! Not those two!" I screamed. "You'll blow up the house!"

4

I snatched up the beaker.

The purple crystals spilled from the test tube and scattered all over the worktable.

"You can't mix chemicals without knowing what will happen, Colin! Those two could have caused an explosion!" I yelled.

"Oh," Colin replied. "Does that mean no stink bomb—just because you're scared of blowing up the house?"

I laughed. I couldn't help it. Like I said, Colin knows how to crack me up.

"Okay, okay. No stink bomb." Colin gave in. "Let's go to the mall."

We started to pack up the chemistry set. "Hey!

What's this?" Colin asked as he tried to shove the test tube rack back into the carton.

He pulled out a single sheet of paper from the bottom of the carton. "Ha! Is this good enough for you?" he exclaimed.

I peered over his shoulder and read the paper. Directions—directions for how to make a stink bomb. Weird.

The instructions were handwritten on a bright orange piece of paper—nothing like the plain white paper the manual was printed on. Very weird.

"Let's do it," Colin urged. "We have all the stuff."

"Well, okay," I finally agreed. How could I pass up the chance to embarrass Michelle?

We measured the chemicals carefully and combined them in a clean beaker. "We'll leave this one out until we're in position upstairs," I told Colin. I showed him a test tube filled with yellow powder.

"Good idea," he answered.

We tiptoed up the stairs and into the kitchen. I peeked into the living room. Jonathan Muller stood by the fireplace, talking about some chess tournament they were organizing.

I spotted Michelle on the sofa. She leaned forward, gazing at Jonathan across the room. The other kids were all focused on Jonathan, too. Perfect.

"Come on," I whispered. I got down on my hands and knees and crawled into the living room. Crawled to the back of the couch and hid behind it. Colin followed.

"Ready?" Colin mouthed, holding out the beaker.

"Yes," I whispered, holding up the test tube. "Hold your breath."

"Don't you mean your *nose?*" Colin snickered.

I snickered, too. Then I poured the yellow powder into the beaker.

We scrunched farther down behind the couch and waited. But nothing happened.

"Take a whiff," I whispered.

Colin put the tube up to his nose. "It doesn't smell at all." He sighed.

"You jerks! What are you doing back there?" Michelle leaned over the back of the sofa, looking meaner than usual. "What is in that beaker, Al?" she demanded.

"It's nothing," I lied. "Honest!"

"You're not supposed to use your chemistry set until *I* show you how," she snapped. "Don't you ever follow directions?"

"But we did follow the directions!" Colin exclaimed, holding up the orange paper. "It's not our fault the stink bomb didn't go off!"

Thanks, Colin, I thought. Thanks a lot.

"You were trying to stink bomb my meeting?" Michelle screeched. "Wait till I tell Mom and Dad. Just wait."

Colin and I took off into the kitchen.

"And leave that chemistry set alone," Michelle called after us.

"Your little brother can't even figure out how to make a stink bomb?" I heard someone say to Michelle. "Are you sure you two are related?"

I felt like a total jerk. Getting caught using the chemistry set was bad enough. But it was worse knowing Michelle and her friends thought I was too dumb to make a stink bomb.

"What should we do with this gunk?" Colin asked when we returned to the basement.

"Throw it out, I guess."

"In the garbage?" Colin asked.

"No, I'll pour it down the sink." I reached for the beaker and noticed that the solution was turning a funny orange color. Neon orange.

"It's working *now?*" Colin groaned.

I smelled the gloppy mess. "No. No, it's not working. It still doesn't stink," I told him.

I placed the beaker on the table. "Let's put the chemistry set away, before my mom gets home. She'll go ballistic if she knows I fooled around with it— without Michelle's help."

"Why bother?" Colin asked. "Michelle's going to tell on you anyway. You know she will."

He had a point. She probably would.

Chester still sat in the corner of the basement. I had forgotten he was even there. He let out a long meow. Then stood up—and leaped onto the table.

20

He strolled toward the beaker, his tail flicking back and forth.

"Shouldn't you be doing your math problems, Chester?" I asked. Chester padded closer to the beaker.

"Off the table. Off!" I gave the cat a little push—and knocked over the stink bomb.

The orange goo poured out. It oozed across the table. Thick and slimy.

Some of it slid over one of Chester's front paws.

All his hair stood straight up.

He arched his back. Flattened his ears.

He hissed at the gooey stuff, baring his sharp white teeth.

Then he leaped off the table, raced up the stairs, and cowered near the door.

"Look at it!" Colin said, amazed. "It's oozing everywhere."

Colin was right. The stuff had oozed across the table. Down the table legs. Onto the floor.

Now it started oozing across the room.

"My mom will kill me if we don't have this stuff cleaned up by the time she gets home!"

I hurried over to the sink and pulled out a big roll of paper towels. I ripped off a long sheet and handed it to Colin.

"Don't get any of it on you," I instructed. "I don't know what these chemicals do to skin."

Colin wrapped the paper towels around his left

hand until it was covered with a wad as big as a catcher's mitt.

Then we went after the ooze.

It didn't soak into the paper towels the way I expected it to. Every time I touched it, it broke into little balls and rolled away.

"This stuff is weird!" Colin exclaimed. "Really weird!"

"Try it like this," I suggested. With a paper towel in each hand, I trapped some ooze between them. Even through the toweling the stuff felt spongy and squishy.

"I'll finish the table. You wipe up the floor," I ordered as I captured another neon-orange glob.

"We're never going to clean up all this gunk! It keeps running away!" Colin made another paper towel catcher's mitt. He crawled across the floor. Trying to wipe up the runny goop.

"We have to," I told him. "We have to clean it up. No way Mom can see this mess. No way!" I opened up a second roll of paper towels and started a fresh attack on the ooze.

We chased the stuff around the room until there was only one puddle left—on the table. It slid away as soon as the paper towel touched it. But I had my other hand ready to stop it.

"Done!" Colin cried. "What should we do with all the paper towels? Flush them?"

I stared at the floor. At the mountain of paper towels heaped there.

"No. No. We can't do that. They'll clog up the toilet," I answered.

"Okay," Colin replied. "I'll just throw them in the garbage."

"No. No. We can't do that, either. They don't pick up garbage until Thursday," I explained. "I don't want any sign of this stuff around."

My eyes searched the basement. I spotted a big red chest—an old cooler that Dad used when he went fishing. Perfect.

"We'll stuff them in here," I said. "And we'd better hurry. Mom will be home any second."

I lifted the top of the chest. It was filled with kitty litter. Bags and bags of kitty litter.

"Al? Are you down there? Al?" Mom called from the top of the basement steps. "I'm home!"

5

"Help me, Colin!" I whispered as I started tossing the bags out.

Click. Click. Click.

The sound of Mom's high-heeled shoes clicked down the basement steps.

"Hurry, Colin. Hurry!"

I gathered up huge bunches of paper towels, careful not to get any of the ooze on my hands.

Chester yowled. "What's wrong, kitty cat?" Mom said on the way down. "It's just me. Nothing to be afraid of."

Mom's heels clicked down the stairs louder— closer.

I yanked the lid off the cooler and crammed the

paper towels inside. Colin shoved his on top and slammed on the lid.

We did it! With my left foot I kicked the cooler under the table—just as Mom stepped into the room. "Having fun?" she asked.

"Just hanging out," I answered, trying to sound normal.

Mom studied me suspiciously. "I see you have the chemistry set out. Did Michelle give you the safety lesson yet, Al?"

"Not yet. But she will," I said. "When the chess club leaves."

Oh, no! I noticed a big drop of the ooze on the worktable. I leaned against the table—trying to look casual. I placed my right hand on top of the orange glob.

"I really don't want you using the chemistry set until you know all the safety rules," Mom warned.

Good. She didn't notice the ooze. "Honest, Mom," I answered. "We were just looking at the test tubes."

I could feel the ooze under my palm. It was growing warm. And it started to slide up between my fingers.

"Okay. If you boys want a snack, there's still plenty of birthday cake left," Mom told us.

The ooze seeped out some more. I slammed my left hand down on top of my right one to cover it. I wasn't going to be able to hide the gooey stuff much longer.

"Awesome, Mrs. Sterner," Colin said. "We will most definitely come up for some cake later."

The ooze started to crawl up through my left hand now. Go, I silently begged my mom. Go upstairs.

"All right," Mom said, and headed back up to the kitchen.

I didn't move until I heard the basement door shut behind her. Then I peered down at my hands. The ooze covered both my palms. And it was spreading up onto my wrists.

"Help me get this gunk off!" I told Colin.

"That stuff is gross," Colin complained. But he made another towel mitt and wiped and wiped— cleaning away the last sign of the weird slimy goo.

When I woke up the next morning, I felt really tired. As if I hadn't slept at all.

I forced myself to sit up. Clothes. What clothes should I wear to school? I couldn't decide. Finally I pulled on a pair of jeans and the first shirt I found when I reached into the closet.

Now I needed socks and shoes. Mom just did the laundry, I remembered. So where did she put my socks?

Forget it, I told myself. I was already running late. The socks I wore yesterday weren't *too* dirty. And they were in my shoes, so I didn't have to hunt all over for them.

I sat down on the bed and pulled on my socks. Then I reached down for a shoe.

I held it for a while, just staring at it. What was

26

wrong with me this morning? Why was I moving so slowly?

I stuffed my foot into the shoe. It felt kind of weird. It didn't hurt exactly. It just felt weird.

"Al, hurry up," Mom called.

I shoved on my other shoe and hurried down the hall. As I walked through the kitchen door, I tripped.

Of course, Michelle didn't miss that one! She laughed so hard she almost choked on her granola.

I looked down to see what I had tripped over, but there was nothing there.

"You idiot!" Michelle laughed as she wiped the tears from her eyes.

"Al could have hurt himself, Michelle!" Mom scolded.

"That's right, Michelle," Dad added. "It's not polite to laugh."

"But his shoes! Look at his shoes!"

"These are the shoes I always wear," I said. "What's wrong with them?"

Dad snorted. I could tell he was trying not to laugh now.

"Oh, my gosh!" Mom exclaimed. "Michelle's right!"

I looked down at my shoes—and gasped!

6

My left shoe was on my right foot!

And my right shoe was on . . . well, I guess you can figure the rest out for yourself.

"No wonder they felt weird," I mumbled. I couldn't believe I had put my shoes on the wrong feet. I must really be tired, I thought.

Feeling a little stupid, I kicked off my shoes and put them on the right feet.

"When are you going to learn to dress yourself, Al?" Michelle teased.

"Now, Michelle," Dad said. "Your brother has been dressing himself since—"

"Since he was ten," Michelle hooted.

"Since he was two," Dad finished.

"Maybe Al better check out summer school—a Getting Dressed for Beginners class," Michelle suggested, still not letting up.

"Has Chester learned any new tricks?" Dad asked, changing the subject to get Michelle off my back. Michelle could talk all day about how smart her cat was.

Chester was snoozing by the stove. "Come here, Chester," Michelle called. "Show Dad how you can add. What is one and one?"

Chester jumped into Michelle's lap and collapsed. "Come on, Chester!" Michelle coaxed. "One and one."

Chester didn't move.

"I'll get a can of cat food," Dad suggested. "That will get him thinking."

Dad slid the can into the electric can opener. "Come on, Chester," he said. "Jump on the lever!"

Chester didn't move.

"I wonder if something is wrong with him." Michelle sounded worried.

"He probably isn't hungry." Dad tried to make her feel better.

Chester might not be hungry. But I was. Hungry and late.

I shoveled down some oatmeal and a piece of toast. Then I grabbed my backpack and headed out the door. "Bye!" I yelled on my way out.

We live only two blocks from Shadyside Middle

29

School. I ran all the way there and made it before the bell rang.

A girl with curly red hair raced up the front steps ahead of me.

"Hey, Al!" I shouted.

She looked over her shoulder. "Hey, Al!" she shouted back at me.

I'm Albert, of course, and her name is Alix. But we kid around, pretending we have the same name. This year we were going to be partners in the Science Bowl.

"You know when Louis Pasteur was born?" I asked.

"1822," she shot back at me. "You know what elements are in water?"

I said the first thing that popped into my head. "Peanut butter and jelly."

She laughed.

"So do you think we'll win?" I asked her.

"Are you kidding?" Alix grinned. "We're the team to beat! No sweat!"

We ran down the hall together and made it to class just as the bell rang.

"Oooh, Al-vin. You almost got a tardy slip," Eric Rice whispered.

He likes to call me Alvin because he thinks it makes me mad. He's a total jerk.

But he's also the toughest kid in the sixth grade. And he sits right behind me. So I try not to get into any arguments with him.

"Who did their memorization?" Miss Scott, our teacher, asked.

All the kids raised their hands. Even Eric. As if he ever does his homework!

I raised my hand, too. Then I realized I couldn't remember what we were supposed to have memorized.

"Who can tell me what the capital of Peru is?" Miss Scott asked, glancing around the class.

As usual Toad waved his hand the hardest. We all called him Toad—even the teachers. But no one could remember how his nickname got started. He was on one of the Science Bowl teams Alix and I would be competing against.

A fly landed on my desk. I watched it rub its front legs over its head again and again.

"How about you, Melanie?" Miss Scott asked.

"It's Lima, isn't it?" Melanie answered.

"Are you asking me or telling me?" Miss Scott replied.

"Well, maybe a little of both," Melanie admitted.

To that fly, I bet my desk is like a huge desert, I thought. I wished I had a little crumb to give it.

"Well, you are right," Miss Scott said. "The capital of Peru is Lima."

"Boy, did she ever luck out," Eric muttered.

Huh? I hadn't really been paying attention.

"Eric?" Miss Scott asked. "Did you have something to add?"

"No, Miss Scott," Eric answered.

"Well, maybe you can tell us the capital of Brazil," Miss Scott said.

There was a pause. We all waited for Eric to say something.

I peered out the window—and noticed some little kids playing dodgeball outside. I used to love to play dodgeball.

"The capital of Brazil, Eric," Miss Scott repeated.

"Now?" Eric asked. "You mean like right now?"

"Well, soon, Eric," Miss Scott said. "The school year ends in June!"

Everyone in the class laughed.

Except Eric, of course.

I kept staring out the window again. That kid in the yellow sweater is going to get creamed, I thought. He is way too slow for dodgeball.

"Eric, the capital of Brazil, please."

"Well, let's see," Eric said slowly.

"You did memorize the capitals over the weekend, didn't you?"

"Oh, sure," Eric said. "Could you repeat the name of the country, please?"

The kids laughed harder.

"Eric, if you didn't study over the weekend, I'll have to ask you to stay after school today," Miss Scott said.

"I have baseball this afternoon," Eric said. "You can't keep me after school today."

Baseball is a good game, too, I thought. Which do I like better—dodgeball or baseball?

"Schoolwork before baseball," Miss Scott declared. "You know the rules, Eric."

There was a knock at the door. Mr. Emerson, the principal, stood in the doorway.

"Excuse me, class," Miss Scott said. "I'll be back in a minute." As soon as Miss Scott joined Mr. Emerson in the hall, Eric turned to me.

"Okay, Al, what's the answer?" he demanded.

"Huh? Answer to what?"

"The capital of Brazil, you jerk," Eric said. "Weren't you listening?"

"Do you think there's going to be another baseball strike?" I asked.

"Come on, Sterner!" Eric hissed. "What is the capital of Brazil?"

"Hot dogs," I said.

"What are you talking about?" Eric demanded.

"I was just thinking that hot dogs taste better at the ballpark than anywhere else. Do you know why?" I asked.

"Tell me the capital of Brazil! Now!" Eric said. I noticed a little vein throbbing in his forehead.

"Oh, it's Cleveland," I whispered just as Miss Scott came back into the classroom.

"Eric?" Miss Scott asked. "What is the capital of Brazil?"

"Cleveland," Eric announced.

33

The whole class laughed. Even Miss Scott had trouble keeping a straight face.

Cleveland? I thought. Why did I say Cleveland?

"Eric," Miss Scott said, "you should plan on staying after school. I see we have our work cut out for us!"

"Cleveland isn't the capital of Brazil?" Eric asked slowly.

"Cleveland is in Ohio," Miss Scott replied. "And it isn't even the capital there!"

I felt Eric's hot breath against my ear. "I'm going to get you for that, Sterner," Eric whispered. "I'm going to get you!"

7

The minute the last bell rang, I jumped out of my chair and raced out the door.

I knew Miss Scott was keeping Eric after school. But I wasn't taking any chances. I wanted to be home—with the door locked—before he even left the building.

I ran down the hall, out the front door, and down the steps. And I kept on running.

I kept hearing Eric's voice in my head. *I'm going to get you for that, Sterner. I'm going to get you.*

And I knew he would.

During math class he passed me a note. A note that mentioned specific bones of my body—and what he planned to do to them.

I thought about the note—and ran faster. I ran three blocks. Four blocks. Five.

My lungs were burning. My legs were aching. But I knew I would feel a lot worse if Eric caught me.

I ran another block—and hit a red light. I glanced behind me as I waited for the light to change.

No Eric yet.

The moment the light turned green I sprinted across the street. Then I stopped.

Wait. There is no stoplight on my way home from school.

I stared around. And I didn't recognize anything. Not anything.

That's impossible, I thought. I have lived in Shadyside my whole life. I should recognize something.

I looked up at the street sign. "Fear Street."

I knew that name. Everybody in Shadyside knew Fear Street. But I couldn't remember ever being on the street before.

I passed house after house. Some were big and fancy. Some were small and run-down. But none of them looked familiar.

Don't panic, I ordered myself. You can't be more than a couple of blocks away from home.

I studied both directions. Which way should I go? If I went the wrong way I might run straight into Eric.

I began to run again. I didn't know where I was headed. But it felt safer to keep running.

Four blocks. Five blocks. Six. Seven. Eight. I ran until there were no more houses—until I hit a dead end.

I could either turn back. Or go into the Fear Street Woods. If I turned back, I might run into Eric, I reasoned.

So I chose the woods. He'd never find me there.

I darted between the trees. They were tall and close together. Hardly any light filtered through their leafy branches. The deeper I walked into the woods, the darker it got.

And it was also getting late. Eric had probably left school by now, I realized.

I heard a rustling sound in the trees behind me. *Oh, no!* I thought. *It's Eric. He found me. I'm dead meat.*

I charged through the trees—and lost my balance. My feet slid out from under me.

I flew through the air, into a clearing, and—splash! I landed up to my knees in water. In a lake—the Fear Street lake.

My shoes were soaked. My feet were freezing.

I sloshed my way up the bank. Climbed out of the water quickly. I had to keep running—no matter how wet my shoes were. No matter how cold my feet felt. No matter what! Because if Eric caught me, he was going to pound me into the ground.

I heard footsteps.

37

I ran faster and faster, but the footsteps were gaining on me. I pumped my legs as hard as I could. My shoes squished as I ran.

But Eric was too fast.

He grabbed my shoulders from behind—and whirled me around.

8

"Hey, where are you going?"

It wasn't Eric! It was Colin!

"Colin, you have to help me!" I cried. "I'm totally lost, and I have to get home before Eric finds me."

Colin gave me a funny look. "We can almost see your house from here." He turned me around and pointed.

He was right. I could see Village Road from where we were standing. I lived on Village Road.

I felt like such an idiot. How could I get lost practically in my own backyard?

"Thanks," I mumbled to Colin. "What are you doing here, anyway?"

"I saw you take off after school. I tried to catch up,

39

but you were too fast. Didn't you hear me calling you?"

"No," I admitted. "I guess I was concentrating on getting away—before Eric found me."

We headed toward my house, not bothering to talk. "You want to come in?" I asked when we reached my front door.

"I can't," he said. "I have to get home. My brother and I are making a music video with my dad's new camcorder. See you tomorrow in school." He started home.

"Okay. Bye," I called. Then I hurried inside—safe from Eric.

I found Michelle sitting at the kitchen table. Her calculus textbook was open in front of her, but she wasn't reading it. She was staring off into space.

"There's something wrong with Chester," Michelle announced. "He's just not himself. He doesn't remember how to use the electric can opener. And he waits for me to turn the TV on for him."

"So what? Maybe he's just lazy," I told her.

"No, Al," she shot back. "You don't get it! There's something really wrong with him. He doesn't know what day of the week it is. He's forgotten how to tell time. He can't even count anymore!" she wailed. "Something happened to him yesterday. I know it. I just know it."

"What makes you think that?" I asked.

"Because he was fine before yesterday," she replied.

I bet no one else in the whole school—maybe even on the whole planet—has a sister who worries about her cat the way she does.

Michelle stared off into space again. Trying to figure out what was wrong with Chester.

"Hey, Tubby!" I yelled. "I'm home. Here, Tubs!" I heard Tubby race down the hall—and into the living room.

"Tubby, I'm in here. In the kitchen," I called.

Tubby woofed.

"Come on, Tubby!"

Tubby woofed again.

"Your dog is so dumb, he can't even make it from the living room to the kitchen without getting lost," Michelle said.

"Yes, he can." I picked up his bowl, poured some dog chow in, and shook the bowl back and forth.

Tubby bounded right into the kitchen. "See?" I said.

"Big deal. He can find his food bowl. Even a goldfish with a teeny, tiny brain can find its food," Michelle cracked.

"Come on, Tubby. We don't have to listen to this. Let's go outside." I marched toward the sliding back door—and walked straight into the glass.

Tubby plowed into it right beside me.

I hope Michelle didn't notice that, I thought.

"Uh, Al," Michelle said.

She noticed.

"Just a suggestion. You might try *opening* the door first next time."

"Ha, ha," I muttered.

"You're getting as dumb as Chester!" she exclaimed. "Quick, Al—how much is one and one?"

I didn't bother to answer. I opened the door and pulled Tubby out into the backyard with me.

I flopped down on the grass. Tubby flopped down beside me.

Something Michelle said bothered me. It wasn't that she called me and Tubby stupid. She does that all the time.

No, it was something she said about her cat. It triggered something in my head. Something I had to figure out—but it wasn't coming to me.

Chester was getting dumb. Is that what she said? No, she said I was getting as dumb as Chester. Were Chester and I getting dumb together?

Something was missing. It was like a jigsaw puzzle, but I couldn't find the next piece. Something happened to Chester yesterday. Hadn't Michelle said that?

Was yesterday my birthday? What happened on my birthday? The opera? No, that wasn't yesterday. No, my birthday was the day before yesterday. Wasn't it? Something happened after my birthday.

Was that yesterday? I remembered smelling something horrible—Michelle's brownies. That must be it!

Michelle's brownies were so bad they did something to my brain.

But wait. I didn't eat a brownie. Chester didn't eat a brownie. Colin ate a brownie. Only he isn't dumber than before. At least I didn't think so.

Focus, I told myself. Focus.

Colin said the brownies stank. No, he didn't! He wanted to make a stink bomb!

Did the stink bomb make me dumb? How could it? It didn't go off! It was a total disaster. It just made a lot of weird orange ooze!

All this thinking was making my head hurt. I felt as though my brain were turning into ooze.

Ooze.

Orange ooze.

What I got all over my hands.

What Chester got all over his paw.

Wait. That's it! Chester and I were getting dumber together. He touched the ooze and now he can't count. I touched the ooze and now I think Cleveland is in Brazil.

The ooze was making us stupid!

I have to talk to Colin, I decided. To run this by him. It seemed to make sense—but I wasn't sure.

I went back inside—without bumping into the glass this time. I ran to my parents' room to use the phone in there. I didn't want Michelle to overhear my conversation.

It took me three tries to get Colin's phone number right. "It's the ooze," I said when he answered.

"What?" Colin asked.

"The ooze," I repeated. Why couldn't he understand me? "The ooze is making me stupid."

"Whoa!" Colin exclaimed. "Who said you're stupid? You're not stupid."

"Yes, I am. I'm stupid—I think."

"Well, you really sound stupid now," Colin said.

"I do?" Boy was I relieved. At least I had something right. "Listen," I told Colin, "Chester stepped into the ooze with his paw. And I touched it with my hand."

"So?" Colin asked.

"So now Chester's as dumb as Tubby. And I got lost on my way home from school. And I walked into a glass door. And I couldn't even remember your telephone number. I'm stupid, Colin! I'm stupid! Chester and I are getting dumb together. And it's all because of the ooze!"

"How could some orange glop do *that?*" Colin asked.

"I don't know! How could I know? It's making me stupid!"

"Okay, okay." Colin tried to calm me down. "I have an idea. Go downstairs and look inside the cooler. Look at the ooze. You'll see. The ooze is just . . . ooze. It can't do anything to you."

"What if it can?" I asked. "What if—"

44

"Just do it," Colin told me.

I hung up and headed for the basement. Colin was right. I had to look at the ooze. See that it was just harmless glop. It was the only thing that would make me feel better.

I opened the basement door and slowly walked down the steps. I spotted the cooler under the table—exactly where I had shoved it.

I raised the lid of the cooler about an inch—and inhaled sharply.

A giant glob of ooze sat on top of the paper towels.

It was as if all the little balls that we had wiped up joined together. Joined into one huge mass of ooze.

And now it was glowing.

I opened the lid a little more—and saw that the glob had veins. *Veins!* Glowing, throbbing veins!

I started to slam the lid down—when the lump of ooze began to bubble. A small bubble broke the surface and popped. Then another. And another.

Bubble. Pop. Bubble. Pop.

More and more tiny bubbles rose to the surface and popped.

Then, without warning, a huge bubble rose up to the surface. It flipped the cooler lid wide open.

I leaped back—back from the growing bubble. But it was too late.

9

Splat!

The giant bubble burst.

A huge glob of the ooze hit my face.

It dripped down my eyes, my nose, my cheeks. It dangled from my chin in a gooey mess.

"Oh, no," I moaned. I was going to be really stupid now.

I had to wash off this horrible stuff right away! Before it made me a total moron.

I scrambled over to the cabinet under the sink. No more paper towels. We used them all yesterday.

I yanked off my T-shirt and started scrubbing my face with it. The ooze was growing warm now. Warm and extra-sticky. I couldn't get it off.

I scrubbed and scrubbed, pressing my lips together tightly. Who knew what would happen if I swallowed some? I certainly didn't—and I didn't want to find out.

My face burned and tingled as I rubbed. But I rubbed furiously until I wiped it all off.

I shoved my T-shirt into the cooler and slammed the lid on. Then I pounded up the basement stairs and down the hall to the bathroom I shared with Michelle. I had to look in the mirror—to make sure not one drop remained.

I locked the bathroom door behind me. Then I leaned as close to the mirror as I could. Searching for even a speck of the orange goo.

I didn't see any. Not a drop. But what if some had seeped into one of my ears—deep inside where I couldn't see it?

I pictured the slimy stuff sliding through my ear—and into my brain! I was doomed.

I have to tell Mom and Dad, I realized. This was a serious problem.

I knew they were going to be angry. I didn't even want to think about what they would do to me. I would probably be grounded until I finished college—if I went to college. I might be way too stupid by then to go.

I had no choice. I had to tell them. I needed their help. They were smart. They did research. Maybe they could figure out a way to save me from a lifetime of stupidity.

My stomach flip-flopped as I headed to the living room to find my parents. They were both sitting on the sofa—reading scientific journals.

I took a deep breath. "Mom, Dad, I have to talk to you," I said. My voice shook only a little.

"What's wrong, dear?" Mom asked. "You look upset."

"It's about the ooze," I started. "Chester and I both touched it. That's why—"

Dad put down his copy of *Biology Today.* "Ooze?" he asked. "What on earth is ooze?"

"Chester stepped in it," I said. "Some of it spilled on the basement table, too. That's how I touched it."

Mom and Dad glanced at each other. I could tell they were confused.

I knew I wasn't explaining things right. But I was confused, too. It was getting hard to keep everything straight in my mind.

"Where did this ooze come from?" Mom asked.

I hesitated. Tell them, I ordered myself. You have to tell them. They are the only ones who can help you.

I opened my mouth to answer—and the doorbell rang.

"I'll get it!" Michelle yelled from the kitchen.

I started to speak again—but Michelle let out a high squeal.

Mom jumped up. "What is it?" she cried. "What is it?"

Michelle practically skipped into the living room. "It's a registered letter from the Eastland Technological Institute!"

I didn't have to ask what that meant. Eastland Technologies has an annual science contest every year for high school students all over the country. You have to be a total brain even to enter. So, of course, Michelle did.

She ripped open the letter. Mom and Dad crowded behind her. Reading over her shoulder.

"You won, honey!" Mom exclaimed. "You won!"

"First prize!" Dad crowed. "We're so proud of you!"

"Mom! Dad!" I pleaded. "I need to talk to you about the ooze! Right now."

"Aren't you going to congratulate your sister?" Mom asked as she reread Michelle's letter.

"Congratulations," I muttered. Michelle didn't bother to answer. "I'm trying to tell you something important," I insisted. "You have to listen. The ooze is why Chester and I have been acting so weird."

"Do you know what I think?" Dad asked.

Yes! I thought. Dad is going to help me!

"What's that, dear?" Mom asked.

"I think we should celebrate," Dad announced. "Let's go someplace really fancy for dinner. It's Michelle's big night."

Thanks a lot, Dad, I thought.

I pulled on Mom's arm. "This is a matter of life and death!" I wailed. "I was playing with the chemistry set and—"

Mom and Dad both turned toward me.

"You played with the chemistry set?" Mom demanded.

"Before Michelle gave you the safety lesson?" Dad added.

I nodded slowly. "And now the ooze is in the cooler and it—"

Mom turned to Dad. "Let's not spoil the celebration for Michelle," she said.

"We'll talk about this tomorrow," Dad told me.

"But I could be so much dumber by then," I protested.

"Dumber? Dumber than using the chemistry set without permission? I don't think so," Mom snapped.

"Get your coat, Michelle," Dad said. "Al, we'll talk about this tomorrow."

I sighed.

Well, maybe going to a restaurant would at least help me get my mind off the ooze. After all, eating was one thing I still knew how to do.

"I'll be right there," I said. "I left my coat in my room."

"Al," Dad called after me, "It's the Science Bowl day after tomorrow."

"Yeah, Dad," I said wearily.

"Do you know how Michelle won her Science Bowls?" Dad asked. "By working hard. By making sacrifices."

Michelle came back with her coat and stood next to Dad. Smirking at me. She was loving every second of this.

"Maybe you should stay home," Dad continued. "You will have the house to yourself—the perfect environment for a good study session."

"But I have to eat, don't I?" I asked.

"You can heat something up in the microwave," Mom said.

"But, Mom . . ." I stopped and shook my head. Nothing I said would make them change their minds. I could see that.

"Have a good time," I muttered as they trooped out the door.

I flopped down on the couch. Now what was I supposed to do? It was clear Mom and Dad weren't going to help me.

Chester strolled into the living room. He jumped up on my lap and started to purr. He liked me a lot more now that he was stupid.

I scratched him under the chin. "What are we going to do? Huh, Chester? I guess you don't know, either."

Tubby came barreling into the room and jumped up on the sofa next to me. "I know *you* haven't got a clue, Tub-man."

51

I sighed and closed my eyes. I pictured my brain filled with orange slime. "Ewwwww!" I cried out. Chester jumped off my lap. Tubby just thumped his tail.

I have to stop the ooze. I can't just sit here all night and let myself get dumber and dumber.

I know! I leaped up from the couch. I'll read the manual that came with the chemistry set. Maybe it would have some answers.

I really didn't want to go back in the basement—at least not alone. So I made Tubby come with me. I didn't even glance at the cooler. I just grabbed the manual out of the box and ran back upstairs.

I raced to my room and slammed the door behind me. Then I sat down at my desk and turned on my reading lamp. Tubby plopped down at my feet.

You can do this, I told myself. I opened the manual to the first page.

"Oh, no!" I groaned. The words were so hard. "Compounds. Elements. Neutralize." How was I supposed to understand big words like that?

Miss Scott would say to look them up in the dictionary. She was always making us look up words.

I pulled my dictionary off the shelf and flipped to the words beginning with the letter C.

I ran my finger down each page. "Com," I muttered. "Com-p. Com-p-oun-d."

Found it. "Composed of or resulting from union of separate elements, ingredients, or parts."

"What does that mean?" I wailed. Okay, okay, don't give up, I told myself. Start with a smaller word.

I flipped to the words beginning with the letter *P*. "Parts," I mumbled. "Parts, parts, parts."

Here it is. "One of the often indefinite or unequal subdivisions . . ."

I slammed the dictionary shut and pounded my head on my desk.

"This is hopeless!" I shouted. "I'm stupid. I'm just too stupid."

Then I had a horrible thought.

How dumb would I be tomorrow?

10

The next morning I didn't have to wonder why I felt so weird. I knew what was wrong. I knew I was dumber. But that was about all I knew.

If I took everything slowly—and didn't say much—I figured I could make it through the day without doing anything too stupid.

I managed to put on jeans and a shirt and my socks. Now came the hard part. My shoes.

I picked up one shoe, flipped it upside down, and studied it. Then I studied my feet. I found a match!

I slipped my shoe on. It felt comfortable.

I didn't even have to think about the other shoe. I stuck it on the other foot and I was set.

You are doing good, I told myself. Very good.

Now I had to brush my teeth and comb my hair. I headed into the bathroom.

I just needed three things—a comb, a toothbrush, and toothpaste. Simple, right?

Well, sort of. It didn't take too long to wash the toothpaste out of my hair.

I rinsed the toothpaste off my comb, put some on my toothbrush, and brushed my teeth.

I didn't bother eating breakfast. I wanted some extra time—in case I got lost on the way to school.

Mom handed me the plastic container with my lunch in it as I headed past her.

"Your dad and I talked about you and the chemistry set last night," she said.

Great, I thought. I have enough to deal with today without a lecture from Mom.

"It was irresponsible of you to use that set without the safety lesson," she told me. "But we know how hard you've been working lately to prepare for the Science Bowl. So we have decided to let you off this time."

Whew! That wasn't bad at all.

"Thanks, Mom," I called. Then I headed out the front door. Concentrating on each step I took, I managed to reach the school before the first bell.

"Hey, Brains!" someone yelled.

I turned and spotted Eric leaning against the big

oak tree in front of school. "Oooooh," I moaned. I had forgotten about Eric.

"You're lucky I didn't find you after school yesterday," he growled.

"Yeah," I muttered, and kept walking.

Eric circled around me and blocked my way. He shoved a piece of paper into my hands.

"What's this?" I asked.

"My math homework," he said. "It's due this afternoon."

"Do you want me to help you with it?" I asked.

"Noooo," Eric crooned. "I want you to do it. And I want it done by lunch!" Then he strutted up the school steps.

I stared down at the paper.

"And do yourself a favor, Sterner," he called back to me.

"What?"

"Do it right," he snarled. "No funny stuff like yesterday. This is your last chance!"

I glanced down at the paper again. I felt my head start to hurt.

Numbers. Lots of them. With math you have to expect that.

But the paper also had tons of strange little symbols on it. They looked familiar. But none of them made any sense to me.

I had to find Colin right away. He knew what was going on. He would help me.

I ran up the front steps, through the double doors, and down the hall. If I reached Miss Scott's room before the final bell rang, I could explain everything to Colin. Then he would do Eric's homework for me! I knew he would!

"Ready for tomorrow?" someone called. Alix trotted up beside me with a big grin on her face.

"Tomorrow?" I asked. "What's tomorrow?"

"As if you didn't know," she teased. "I bet you have been studying for the Science Bowl nonstop. Admit it, Al. You don't want everyone around here to say your sister is smarter than you are."

"I guess not," I mumbled. "I guess not."

The bell rang as soon as we walked through the door. Miss Scott started the class immediately.

No time to talk to Colin.

Now what was I going to do?

Eric was expecting his math homework at lunch. And I wouldn't be able to talk to Colin before then.

I guess I'll have to try it by myself, I thought. I stared down at the assignment. Studying it as hard as I could.

What did that little cross mean? And what was that line with the dot above and below it?

I could feel Eric's hot breath on the back of my neck. I'll never figure this out. Never. He's going to kill me.

The hours until lunch passed so quickly—I could hardly believe it when the bell rang. "I'll be waiting

57

right outside the door for my homework, Brains!" Eric growled.

I carefully returned my books to my backpack. I gathered all my pens together and put a rubber band around them. I organized my pencils, then I brushed the pink fuzz off my big eraser.

How long would Eric wait for me? Would he give up and go to lunch? Or would he guard the door until I got there?

"Al?" Miss Scott asked. "Aren't you hungry?"

I glanced around the room. All the other kids were gone. "Not especially," I said. "Do you know where the sponge is? I want to wash the top of my desk."

"Later, Al," Miss Scott said. "Go to lunch now, even if you aren't hungry. It's an order. Go to lunch."

When I stood up, my legs started to tremble. But I had no choice. I had to walk out that door.

"Hand it over!" Eric barked the second I stepped into the hall.

"I didn't . . ." I mumbled. "I couldn't."

"Wrong answer, Al-vin." Before I could say another word, he lunged at me.

He grabbed the back of my shirt, but I jerked free. I took off toward the cafeteria. When I reached the double doors, I spun right and ran down another hall.

A group of fifth graders swarmed down the stairs. I pushed my way into the crowd, taking the stairs two and three at a time.

"Hey, use the other stairs!" one of the kids shouted.

"Don't you know this is the down staircase?" another kid yelled. "What are you, a moron?"

I didn't bother to answer.

I plowed through those kids all the way to the next floor.

I glanced over my shoulder. Eric stood at the bottom of the stairway, trying to fight his way up.

"I'm coming for you, Sterner!" he shouted.

I bolted down the hall until I came to another staircase. It was the up staircase, but I ran down it as fast as I could. Before anybody could stop me, I raced straight out of the school.

I didn't stop running until I reached home. Mom and Dad were both at work. Michelle was still in school.

What am I going to do? I thought. What am I going to do? I have to figure out something.

But I can't, I realized. I just can't. I couldn't even do a simple math problem anymore. How could I figure out what to do about the ooze—a much bigger problem. Much bigger.

There was no way I could.

I was just too dumb.

And getting dumber every second.

"Al! Wake up!" Dad called. "It's Science Bowl day!"

I didn't want to wake up. I didn't want to go to school. And I definitely didn't want to be in the Science Bowl.

I rolled onto my stomach and buried my head under my pillow.

I heard Dad open my door. "Al, get moving. Do you know what time it is?"

I opened my eyes and stared at the alarm clock. The little hand was on the seven and the big hand was on the two.

But what did that mean?

I couldn't remember how to tell time.

I sat up, rubbed my eyes, and stared at the clock

60

again. I still had no idea what it said. How could I forget something I learned back in kindergarten? I was stupider than ever!

Dad walked over and sat down on the bed next to me. "Better step on it, Al. You need to be sharp if you expect to shine at the Science Bowl this afternoon!"

"But, Dad, I really don't feel . . ." I began.

But he wasn't listening. "You need to have a good breakfast. That's very important. And you need to find a few minutes before the Science Bowl to give yourself a mental pep talk," Dad instructed.

"Mmm-hmm," I mumbled.

"I know you'll do great. Just like your sister!" Dad clapped me on the back and left the room.

I thought I was doing great when I was able to get dressed, brush my teeth, and comb my hair with no mistakes. But I knew it would take a lot more than that to please Dad.

I shuffled into the kitchen and plopped down in my chair.

Michelle grinned her horrible grin at me. "Ready for the big day?" she chirped.

I grunted. What could I say?

My mom set a plate of scrambled eggs and bacon down in front of me. "Protein is good brain food," she said.

I knew I needed a lot more than protein to get through the Science Bowl—without the whole school laughing at me. I needed a miracle.

"Let me quiz you," Michelle suggested. She picked up my *Science Teasers* book.

"You mind if I eat first?" I grumbled.

"I'm trying to help you build up your confidence," Michelle pouted. "It's how *I* won all the Science Bowls *I* was ever in."

Michelle thumbed through the book. "We'll start with an easy one. Here's an astronomy question. What was Galileo's earth-shaking discovery?"

I had no idea.

I shoveled a huge forkful of scrambled egg into my mouth, hoping I would come up with an answer before I swallowed.

I didn't.

"Come on, Al," Dad urged. "Just give her the answer."

"I'm hungry," I complained. "I don't want to be quizzed now."

"I was only trying to help," Michelle whined.

Mom ruffled my hair. I hate that. It makes me feel like such a baby. "He's probably nervous. It's his first Science Bowl, after all."

"I'll give you a hint," Dad said. "It has to do with what you are to me."

I spooned some jelly on my toast and took a huge bite. Think, I told myself with each chew. Think, think, think. What was I to Dad? His kid. What could that have to do with Galileo?

62

"Now I'll give you a hint," Michelle volunteered. "It doesn't have to do with what I am to Dad."

Michelle's hint only made me more confused. Why wouldn't they leave me alone?

"You can do it, *son*," Dad said.

I tried to smile at him. But I had no idea what the answer was. Galileo. Galileo. It sounded like the name of one of those Teenage Mutant Ninja Turtles.

"The *sun* sure is bright today," Michelle said. "I love the *sun*. Don't you, Al?"

I drank my whole glass of orange juice without taking a breath. But when I set my glass down, Mom, Dad, and Michelle were staring at me. Waiting for my answer.

Michelle shook her head in disgust and shoved *Science Teasers* back over to me. "Galileo's earth-shaking discovery was that the earth revolves around the *sun.*" She said each word slowly and clearly.

I pretended not to hear her. I pretended to study *Science Teasers* so my family would lay off. But I could only understand a couple of words on every page.

"You want to make Mom and Dad proud, don't you?" Michelle asked. She never gives up. "And don't forget Mr. Gosling. You want him to be proud, too, don't you?"

Mr. Gosling was my science teacher. I felt my head start to throb. What Michelle said made me think of something. Something important. But what?

Mr. Gosling, I thought. Something about Mr. Gosling.

What do I know about him? Not much. He's smart. I know that, I thought.

That's it. *He* is smart. *He* isn't getting stupider and stupider. If I show the ooze to him, maybe he can help me!

I finished the rest of my breakfast as fast as I could. I stuck my plate and orange juice glass in the dishwasher, but I stuck my spoon in my pocket.

I spotted the plastic container Mom kept her coupons in on the counter. Perfect. When no one was looking, I emptied the coupons into a drawer and stuck the container under my shirt.

"Be right back," I announced. "I left my notebook in the basement."

The cooler was still under the table, just where I left it. I opened the lid. Only a crack. I couldn't let the ooze splash me—the way it did the day before. I couldn't afford to get any stupider.

I peeked into the cooler. Whoa! The ooze had grown. And it had more veins. Lots more throbbing veins.

My heart pounded as I stared at the disgusting glob.

I started to jab the spoon in—but the ooze jerked away from it. It moved from the spoon—before the spoon even touched it.

I slammed down the lid and jumped back in fear.

This stuff was disgusting *and* creepy. Totally creepy.

My hands started to tremble as I inched toward the cooler again. Don't think about it, I told myself. Just scoop some up. All you need is a little bit on the spoon.

I opened the lid again, shoved the spoon deep into the quivering mass, and dropped a blob of it into the container.

I clamped the lid on and made sure it was sealed tightly. Then I smuggled the ooze back upstairs and slid it into my backpack.

"Wish me luck," I said as I slipped the backpack over my shoulder.

"Good luck." Michelle laughed. "You're really going to need it!"

Mom gave me a hug and my plastic lunch container with a sandwich inside. "Good luck, Al!"

Dad shook my hand. "We'll be in the audience cheering you on!" he said.

I nodded. And as I walked to school, I tried not to think about my parents . . . watching me in horror . . . as I gave one wrong answer after another in the Science Bowl.

Alix and Colin were waiting for me on the school steps. "You ready for the big day, Al?" Alix asked.

"I studied for it," I said. That was true. And it was better than telling Alix she now had an idiot for a Science Bowl partner.

"I'm betting on both of you!" Colin told us as we headed toward Miss Scott's class.

Eric was already there when we walked through the door. And he did not look happy.

I carefully slid my backpack under my seat and pretended not to notice him.

"I flunked the math homework," Eric told me. "You know what that means?"

I shrugged.

He poked me in the back. "That means I had to stay after school again. And you know what that means?"

I shook my head. Why was he asking me so many questions?

He poked me in the back again. "That means I had to miss baseball practice again. No one makes me miss practice and gets away with it, Sterner! No one." Poke. Poke. Poke.

"I couldn't figure out the problems, okay?" I blurted out. "I'm not smart enough."

"Oh, yeah. Right," Eric shot back. "I'm going to get you, Brains. You can count on it. . . ."

Wrong, Eric, I thought. I don't know how to count anymore.

Eric would have gone on and on, but Miss Scott

entered the room. She paused by my desk. "Are you feeling better today, Al?"

Huh? Why was she asking me that? She didn't know about the ooze. Did she?

"You left school early yesterday," she reminded me when I didn't answer. "I hope you're feeling well enough for the Science Bowl this afternoon."

Oh, yeah, I thought. I did leave early yesterday. "I'm okay," I mumbled.

Miss Scott continued up to her desk. "You aren't going to be okay when the lunch bell rings," Eric whispered. "When I catch up with you, you are going to be very dead meat."

I didn't bother trying to follow Miss Scott's social studies lesson. Or the grammar lesson after that. I just kept my eyes focused on the top of my desk and hoped she wouldn't call on me.

Eric never let me forget for a second that he was going to get me. He dropped his pencil next to my desk and muttered "meat" when he bent down to pick it up. He threw a tiny note over my shoulder that said *"very* dead meat."

The morning crawled by. But finally it was almost lunchtime.

At least I thought it was. The big hand and the little hand of the clock were both straight up.

"Who can tell me what the direct object is in this sentence?" Miss Scott pointed to the chalkboard.

Don't look at her. Don't move a muscle, I told myself.

"Al?" Miss Scott called.

"Al?" Miss Scott said again. "The direct object?"

Eric snickered.

I felt my hands start to sweat. My throat tightened up.

Then the intercom crackled. "Will the contestants in this afternoon's Science Bowl please meet in the library," the school secretary said over the speaker. "Mr. Emerson would like to have a brief meeting with you before lunch."

Saved! At least for now. I grabbed my backpack and hurried out of the room with Alix and Toad.

The other Science Bowl kids—Melanie, Tanya, and Geoff—met us in the hall.

Mr. Emerson kept us in the library for only a few minutes. He went over the rules of the Science Bowl and told us we were all winners just for competing.

Tell that to my parents, I thought. Or Michelle.

The six of us trooped down to the cafeteria together. "Let's sit at the same table," Alix suggested. We didn't usually eat with each other, but today everyone seemed to feel like it.

I know I did. Even Eric wouldn't try to drag me away from five other kids. At least I hoped he wouldn't.

"I'm too nervous to eat," Tanya said as she sat down next to me.

What does she have to be nervous about? I thought. She doesn't have ooze for brains.

"Not me!" Alix insisted. "Al and I are ready. You guys better watch out."

Yeah, right. Poor Alix. It's not fair that she's stuck with me for a partner. Poor Alix.

I pulled out my lunch and opened the plastic container.

"No way you guys are going to win," Geoff shot back. "Toad and I had a three-day study marathon. Friday, Saturday, Sunday. He slept over and we quizzed each other nonstop."

"What's that?" Toad asked me.

"What?" I asked. Then I looked down and gasped. I opened the wrong container. It wasn't my lunch container. It was the container with the ooze.

And the little spoonful I plopped in this morning had grown. It filled every inch of the container now.

"Let me see," Alix said.

"No!" I shouted. "No," I repeated more softly. "I mean it isn't food. It's . . . it's . . . nothing."

"It looks like something to me," Alix teased.

I shoved the lid on the container and tried to stuff it in my backpack.

But Alix was too fast.

She lunged across the table.

She grabbed the container right out of my hands, ripped off the lid, and plunged her fingers inside.

12

_~~~_

"**N**oooo!" I shrieked. "Nooooo!"

"Hey, I'm your partner!" Alix said. "You have to share with me. I love this Super Slime stuff. My sister got some for Christmas."

I tried to wrestle the ooze from her. But she held it over her head. "I want to play with it, Al. Pleeease."

She grabbed a handful of the orange gunk.

"I want some, too!" Geoff grabbed the container from Alix and scooped out some more.

"Give it back, guys," I begged. "Please give it back!" But no one paid attention to me.

"Hey, don't forget about the Green Team. Melanie and I want some slime!" Tanya cried.

Geoff tossed the container to Tanya. She shoved both hands into the ooze and made a ball.

"Tanya! Give it to me!" I shouted. "You don't know what that stuff is!"

"Of course we know what it is," Melanie declared. "I want some, too."

Tanya slid the ooze over to Melanie. She pulled out a handful. "Want some, Toad?"

"Yeah!" Toad answered.

"Please. Please. Please. Give it to me!" I wailed.

"Sure," Geoff said. He threw a wad of the ooze at me. But he missed, and it hit Tanya right in the forehead.

Tanya loaded her plastic spoon with a mound of the stuff. She bent the spoon backward, then let it go— launching a gob at Geoff. Splat! A direct hit.

"This stuff is so cool!" Tanya exclaimed. "And I love the color. I've never seen this color before. I bet it glows in the dark."

"Give it back," I chanted. "Give it back. Give it back. Give it back."

Toad gave a huge fake sneeze—and pretended that a big gob of ooze flew out of his nose.

"Gross!" Alix yelled.

"That's not gross," Toad said. "This is gross!" He rubbed some of the ooze in Geoff's hair.

Melanie pointed at Geoff's hair and started giggling. She giggled so hard she couldn't talk. Then everyone threw some ooze at Melanie. Everyone except me, of course.

I stared around the table. It was an all-out ooze fight.

Globs of the neon stuff ran down their foreheads and their cheeks. Clumps of it nested in their hair and stuck to their hands.

It was hopeless. Totally hopeless.

They were all going to turn as dumb as I was!

13

"**W**hy won't anyone talk to me?" I asked Alix.

"Because you made such a big deal about the slime. Next time don't be so selfish," Alix said as we headed toward the auditorium. "Then you won't make anyone mad. It's as simple as two plus two equals . . ."

I stopped and faced her. "Equals what?" I asked. "Equals what, Alix?"

I still knew the answer to two plus two. But did Alix? How stupid had the ooze made her?

"Two plus two," Alix mumbled. She frowned. "Two plus two . . ."

You can do it, Alix, I thought. Come on. Two plus two equals twenty-two. You know this.

"What is two plus two?" I repeated.

Alix giggled. "I can't remember. I must be too nervous about the Science Bowl." She smiled at me. "Don't worry, partner," she said. "I'll be fine once it starts."

But I knew the truth. Alix wouldn't be fine. The ooze had definitely drenched her brain.

As we continued down the corridor, I spotted my mom and dad outside the auditorium.

"We wanted to say good luck, honey," Mom called, "before the Bowl starts."

I tried to smile as we walked up to my parents, but I was having a hard enough time breathing.

"Good luck, son," Dad said, slapping me on the shoulder.

"Thanks, Dad," I said. "Thanks."

I peeked into the auditorium. Almost every seat was taken. My throat went dry.

"Let's go," Alix urged. "It's about to begin."

"I know you won't let us down," Mom said.

I waved to my mom and dad and followed Alix into the auditorium. Toad grinned at me as we climbed up onto the stage. "You are going to lose," he mouthed. But Geoff looked a little nervous.

Alix and I sat down at the empty table. I glanced over at Melanie and Tanya. Neither of them appeared nervous at all.

Melanie was blowing a huge, pink, bubble-gum

bubble. Tanya was staring at it as it grew bigger and bigger.

Mr. Emerson stepped out onstage just as Melanie's bubble popped. He glared at her as she pulled pieces of gum off her face.

"Welcome to the first round of this year's Science Bowl!" Mr. Emerson announced. "I want to welcome the students, the faculty, the friends, and the families in our audience. I also want to congratulate our contestants in advance. No matter what happens today, they are all winners!"

I doubted Mr. Emerson would still feel that way when the Science Bowl was over. I knew my family wouldn't.

"Let's start," Mr. Emerson said. "Remember— when one team misses a question, the other teams get a chance at it. Good luck to all of you."

He smiled broadly and took a wad of index cards from his pocket. "We'll start with the Blue Team," he announced.

Whew! At least my team didn't get the first question. "With all the talk about genes these days," Mr. Emerson read, "tell us what the letters in DNA stand for."

Geoff stared at Toad. Toad stared at Geoff.

"Well, don't both jump in at once," Mr. Emerson said, laughing.

How dumb were Toad and Geoff now? Would one of them be able to get the right answer?

"DNA?" Toad asked. "You better take it, Geoff."

"No," Geoff whispered. "You take it. You're always bragging about how smart you are. So prove it."

Toad shook his head. "It wouldn't be fair for me to answer *all* the questions."

Reluctantly Geoff stood up. "DNA," he mumbled. "That's a hard one."

"I'll give you a hint," Mr. Emerson said. "It has to do with genetics."

Geoff stared at the floor. "It sounds familiar." He sighed. "I heard about genetics *somewhere.*"

Why did I have to bring the ooze to school with me? Why? Why? Why? Geoff's brain was pudding—and it was all my fault!

"I can't remember," Geoff finally admitted.

Mr. Emerson turned to Melanie and Tanya. "Anyone on the Green Team want to take a crack at it?" he asked.

Maybe one of them still had enough brainpower to get the right answer. I knew I didn't.

Melanie pulled a piece of gum off her nose and popped it into her mouth. "I don't think so," she said, chewing her gum nervously.

I noticed my parents in the front row. Dad gave me a big thumbs-up. He probably figures I have it made—now that the other teams missed the question, I realized.

"Red Team?" Mr. Emerson asked. He sounded a little worried.

76

I glanced over at Alix. She was muttering "DNA" over and over—and shaking her head back and forth.

"We don't know, either," I told Mr. Emerson.

Someone in the crowd laughed. I thought it was Eric, but I didn't look. I didn't want to see anyone in the audience—especially my dad. He wouldn't be giving me the thumbs-up now.

"Well, maybe we should move on to a different area of scientific investigation," Mr. Emerson said stiffly.

He pulled another card out of his stack. "This is for the Red Team," Mr. Emerson announced. "What is the definition of *ecology?*"

"I know!" Alix cried. She jumped to her feet.

Maybe the ooze hadn't hurt Alix as much as I thought!

"Wonderful, Alix!" Mr. Emerson exclaimed. "Tell us what ecology is."

The big smile on Alix's face turned into a frown.

"Alix?" Mr. Emerson prompted.

"I knew a second ago," she said, biting her bottom lip.

I could hear people in the audience whispering to each other. And a couple kids laughing.

Alix balled her hands into fists. "I *did* know the answer. I did! I did!"

"You'll have another chance, Alix," Mr. Emerson said. "Science Bowls can be tense, can't they? Now, would the Blue Team like to answer the question?"

Geoff pointed to Toad.

77

"What was the question again?" Toad asked.

Mr. Emerson sighed. "What is ecology?" he repeated.

Toad stood up with his shoulders back and his head up. "Ecology is how much money people make and what they spend it on," Toad said loudly.

"That is incorrect," Mr. Emerson told him.

"Are you sure?" Toad asked.

"What?" Mr. Emerson asked in disbelief.

"Check the answer!" Toad insisted. "My dad's an ecologist—so I know I got it right!"

"I'm an economist! An economist!" a man yelled from the back of the auditorium.

"Are you sure, Dad?" Toad began. "I thought—"

"Toad!" Mr. Emerson interrupted. "Please sit down. The answer is incorrect."

Mr. Emerson turned to Tanya and Melanie. "Girls?" he asked. "Want to give it a try?"

Melanie twisted her charm bracelet around her wrist. "Isn't Ecology the name of that bear who says 'Only you can prevent forest fires'?"

"No, it is not," Mr. Emerson said. I could see sweat shining on his face. "It is not even close."

"Next question. For the Green Team. What year was Louis Pasteur born?"

"Who?" Tanya asked.

"Huh?" Melanie said.

"Red Team?" Mr. Emerson pulled out a handker-

78

chief and wiped off his forehead while he waited for me and Alix.

Alix shook her head. She brushed the back of her hand across her eyes.

I felt my stomach knot. Was Alix crying? She never cried.

"I'm letting everyone down, aren't I?" Alix exclaimed. "I shouldn't be in the Science Bowl. I'm not smart enough."

"Neither is Geoff," Toad interrupted. "He lost us the DNA question."

"You didn't know the answer, either!" Geoff yelled.

"Did, too!" Toad shot back.

"Did not!" Geoff answered. "And you thought your dad was an ecologist!"

"He is an ecologist!" Toad said.

"Is not!" Geoff growled.

"That is enough!" Mr. Emerson snapped.

"Is, too," I heard Toad whisper.

Melanie and Tanya weren't paying any attention to Toad and Geoff or Alix or Mr. Emerson. Melanie had another huge bubble going. And Tanya started braiding her hair.

"I don't even know what two plus two is!" Alix suddenly cried out. "Something's wrong with me! I let you down, Al! I'm sorry!" Then she ran off the stage.

I leaped up and started after her. "Stop, Alix!" I shouted. "It's not your fault. It's my—"

Mr. Emerson grabbed my arm. "One of the teachers will see to Alix," he told me. "Sit down!"

I sat.

"Let's try another question," Mr. Emerson said in a shaky voice. "This is for the Blue Team. Who discovered that the earth revolves around the sun?"

The sun. That reminded me of something. Breakfast—Michelle quizzing me.

"Toad? Geoff? Do either of you know the answer?"

"I don't want to be on his team anymore!" Geoff blurted out.

"Well, I don't want you on my team!" Toad answered.

"Stop!" Mr. Emerson shouted. He closed his eyes for a long moment. "Stop," he said more quietly. "Would the Green Team like to answer?"

Melanie raised her hand.

"Yes, Melanie!" Mr. Emerson sounded so happy.

"Can I get some more gum? I think better when I'm chewing gum, and I just swallowed mine," Melanie said.

Everyone in the audience laughed. I couldn't wait to get off the stage. I couldn't wait for the Science Bowl to end.

"No, you may not have more gum," Mr. Emerson said firmly. I could see a little muscle twitching near his left eye.

"Then I can't answer the question," Melanie replied.

"Tanya?" Mr. Emerson said.

Tanya jerked her head up. "Huh?"

Mr. Emerson shook his head. "Anyone? Can *anyone* tell me who discovered that the earth rotates around the sun?"

I glanced out into the auditorium. My parents were both nodding and smiling at me.

Wait. Wait. I knew this.

I pressed my hands against the sides of my head. If I pressed hard enough, maybe the answer would come out of my mouth.

Something about my dad? No, something about a Teenage Mutant Ninja Turtle.

"Galileo!" I exclaimed.

A big smile broke out on Mr. Emerson's face. The audience burst into applause. My mom and dad clapped the hardest.

I scored the first point in the Science Bowl!

14

Unfortunately, it was also the *last* point anyone scored in the Science Bowl.

Mr. Emerson asked three more questions—and no one even tried to answer them.

Geoff and Toad got into a shouting match over who was stupider. All Melanie would talk about was gum. And Tanya kept trying out new hairstyles.

Finally Mr. Emerson threw his stack of questions on the floor. "I don't know what's wrong with you!" he cried. "We have always had outstanding students in the Science Bowl! You are all bright kids. Just what kind of stunt are you trying to pull?"

"I studied," Toad protested. "Every night. I knew all this stuff before lunch!"

But Mr. Emerson wouldn't listen. I had never seen him so angry. "The Science Bowl is over," he declared. "This school will not hold another one until the students are able to convince me that they are mature enough to take part."

Most of the kids and teachers and parents filed out of the auditorium quickly and quietly. But my parents waited for me at the edge of the stage.

I walked slowly down the steps and followed them out of the school. I didn't know what to say to them.

None of us spoke until we were a block away from home. Then my father broke the silence. "I don't understand what happened today. You aren't dumb, Al," he said.

"I knew Galileo, didn't I?" I mumbled. "I got more points than anyone else, didn't I?"

"But you should have been able to answer every question," Dad replied.

"I'm disappointed in Al's performance, too," my mother said. "But all the kids had a difficult time this afternoon. It was their first Science Bowl. They were all nervous."

"Michelle did brilliantly in her first Science Bowl," my father pointed out. "A little nervousness gets the juices flowing—as long as you know your stuff. And Al obviously didn't."

We turned into our driveway. "Your father and I have to go back to work," my mother said. "You stay in your room and think about what happened this afternoon. We'll talk about it when we get home."

"We have to make sure this never happens again," my father added. "If you aren't careful, you'll ruin your chances of getting into a good college."

College! I probably wouldn't make it through the sixth grade after what the ooze had done to me.

I watched my parents climb in their cars and drive off. Then I headed up to the house. I turned the doorknob and pulled. The door wouldn't open.

I pulled on it again—as hard as I could. It still wouldn't open.

Then I turned the doorknob and *pushed.* The door flew open and I stumbled inside.

My pulse thudded in my ears. I could hardly remember how to open a door. What was I going to do?

I walked down the hall to my room and sat down on my bed. Tubby wandered in and jumped up next to me.

I noticed a magazine on my nightstand. It had a photo of a pair of in-line skates on the cover. I tried to read the name of the magazine. But after the *S* I gave up and threw the magazine on the floor.

I flopped back on my bed and stared at the ceiling. The ooze had destroyed my life. I couldn't read. I couldn't think clearly. I couldn't open a door.

Mr. Emerson was furious at me. My science teacher, Mr. Gosling, probably felt humiliated.

And my parents—my parents thought I was a total loser.

I didn't even want to think about what Michelle would say to me when she heard how I blew it at the Science Bowl.

But here was the worst thing—four other kids touched the ooze. Their lives would be ruined, too. And it was all my fault.

How stupid were we going to get? I wondered.

I decided I really didn't want to think about it anymore.

I didn't want to think about what else could happen to us before the ooze completely destroyed our brains.

I didn't want to think about it—because I had absolutely no way to stop it.

15

Buzz.

I sat up in bed and listened.

Buzz. There it was again.

I should do something when I hear that sound. But what?

Buzz. Buzz. Buzz.

I left my room and followed the noise—to the front door.

"Al, let me in!"

It was Colin.

The doorbell. That's what the buzzing sound was—the doorbell. And when you hear the doorbell, you open the door, I told myself.

I pulled open the front door—on the first try!—and

Colin rushed in. His face was red and sweaty. He must have run all the way from school.

"It was the ooze, wasn't it?" Colin asked, panting.

I nodded. "Everyone in the Science Bowl touched it. Now they're dumb, too."

"What are you going to do?" Colin exclaimed.

"I don't know," I moaned. "I have to find some way to get our brains back. But I'm too stupid to figure out how!"

"Don't worry," Colin said. "I'll help you."

What could Colin do? He was smarter than I was now. But that didn't make him smart enough to solve this problem.

"We have to kill the ooze," Colin declared.

"Wait," I said. I knew there was something wrong with that idea. But what? "Wait. If you kill the ooze . . . maybe you would kill our brains with it."

"Oh, yeah," Colin answered. He shut his eyes. His forehead wrinkled as he thought.

Then his eyelids popped open and he smiled. "I have a plan. We have to, um, what's that word? I know I got it right on the science quiz."

"Don't ask me," I told him.

"Neutralize!" Colin burst out. "That's it. We have to *neutralize* the ooze."

"Neutralize?" I repeated. That word sounded familiar. But I had no idea what it meant.

"We find a chemical and add it to the ooze, and then the ooze loses its power," Colin explained.

"Maybe if you touch it after we neutralize it, you'll get your brains back. Come on. Let's go down to the basement."

What Colin said seemed to make sense—but, then, what did I know? I was stupid.

"The first thing we'll do is get a little piece of the ooze," Colin said, racing down the basement steps. "Then we can try different chemicals on it until we figure out what will neutralize it."

Colin hurried over to the cooler. He dragged it from under the table. Then he reached for the lid.

"Stop!" I yelled. "Open it only a little," I warned him.

"Okay, okay," he replied. He opened the lid a crack.

Thud-thud. Thud-thud.

What was that? It was a familiar sound, I knew that. One I'd heard a million times.

Thud-thud. Thud-thud.

A heartbeat! That's it! A heartbeat!

But it wasn't my heartbeat.

I broke out into a cold sweat.

I inched up behind Colin. He opened the lid a little wider. I leaned down and peered inside.

Deep in the center of the ooze I saw it. A heart. Bigger than my fist. Much bigger. With tangles of thick twisted veins running through it.

The hideous heart pumped and pumped. The huge veins throbbed with every *thud-thud.*

"A heart!" Colin gasped. "It grew a heart!"

Bam!

Without warning, the ooze exploded out of the cooler in a giant wave. It crashed against the lid, sending it flying across the room.

Colin jerked me back as the quivering orange mass sprang from the cooler. It landed on the floor in front of us with a horrible plop.

Then it started to grow. And grow.

It grew so fast, we could see it happening.

"H-how is it doing that?" Colin stammered.

"I-I don't know," I replied. "But it's not stopping."

The ooze stood at least four feet high now. A big orange mound—shaking and rolling.

We backed up. The ooze shimmied forward.

Does it know we're here? Can it sense us somehow?

I took another step backward and—*screech!* I stepped on Chester. I didn't even know he was down here with us.

Chester raced past me—and headed straight for the ooze.

"Chester, no!" I screamed. "No!"

The cat skidded to a stop inches away from the slime. He whirled around.

But he wasn't fast enough. The ooze rose in another wave. Then it crashed over Chester—and trapped him inside its quivering walls.

I watched in horror as Chester tried to fight his way

89

out. The ooze bulged and stretched as he slammed against it.

One of his claws slashed through the slime. But the ooze quickly sucked it in again.

Then Chester's head broke free. He twisted and jerked, struggling to push his body out of the throbbing trap.

I lunged toward the cat—to try to pull him out.

Colin grabbed my arm. "Don't!" he ordered. "You can't help him. The ooze will get you, too!"

Chester uttered a long wail that made the hair on my arms stand straight up. I could hardly watch as the ooze spread back up over Chester's head. Over his eyes. His nose. His mouth.

Chester gave a last strangled yowl as the ooze let out a horrible slurping sound. Then Chester was gone.

Smothered by the ooze. Totally smothered.

My knees trembled hard. I pressed myself against the wall so I wouldn't collapse.

My eyes remained glued to the quivering mass as it slowly slid across the floor, slithering right by us.

"Hey! Look!" I cried out. "Look!"

The ooze left a slimy trail in front of us. And in the middle of it sat Chester.

It let him go! It let him go! Chester was alive!

"Here, Chester!" I called.

Chester didn't move.

"Come here, kitty-kitty," I urged. "You're okay now."

90

Chester just sat there. Staring into space with his mouth hanging open. He looked totally out of it—dumbstruck.

Dumbstruck!

"Oh, no!" I moaned when I realized the truth. "Oh, no! Chester's completely dumb. Completely dumb! The ooze sucked out *all* of Chester's brain! *All of it!*"

"Look!" Colin croaked, pointing to the horrible slime.

The ooze had stopped in its tracks.

It began to shake really hard now.

"It's going to explode!" Colin screamed. "It's going to explode! Run! Run!"

But I couldn't run. I couldn't move. I could only stare at the horrible ooze, shaking wildly now—and starting to stretch! Stretching straight up. Higher and higher.

My jaw dropped as it grew. I could see its hideous heart, hammering away, as it rose up, taller and taller. Ten feet tall now.

Then, with a sickening *thwack*, two huge bubbles appeared on each side of it.

They began to stretch, too—stretch out. Out to the sides. Out, out, out.

"Wh-what's it doing?" Colin stammered.

"I-I think it's growing arms." I gaped in fear. "It—it is. It's growing arms!"

"Oh, no," Colin croaked. "Hands, too."

Hands. Two wet, glowing hands sprang out from the long, moist arms.

And then we both gasped—as eight fingers grew from each hand. Long, glowing fingers that began to snake out.

Snake toward us.

Reaching. Reaching. Reaching—for our throats.

16

"Nooooo!" I screamed. "Nooooo!"

The ooze's glowing fingers stretched until they were inches from my face. Then they stopped.

Colin grabbed my arm and pointed to the creature's body. "I don't think it can move now that it's changed shape," he whispered. "I think it's stuck to the floor."

I stared at the neon-orange body. Colin was right. The bottom of the ooze was rooted to its spot. Its hands couldn't reach any closer.

"Let's get out of here!" I cried. "Now!"

Colin and I edged away from the ooze. I trained my eyes on the creature—careful to stay out of its grasp.

Then I froze in horror.

93

"L-look, Colin. Look." A round bubble was forming on the top of the ooze. "It—it's growing a head."

My heart pounded as the bubble grew and grew, then tore open in two spots—forming empty, staring eyes.

With another rip a huge hole opened, forming a hideous, gaping mouth.

But the worst part was the brain.

The ooze had a massive brain.

I could see it pushing, pulsating against the top of the creature's head. Straining against its slimy skull.

"Come on!" Colin yanked on my arm. "Let's go!"

But I didn't move.

I stood there—frozen. And watched as the horrible ooze creature began to grow legs.

"Run!" Colin screamed. "Run!" He grabbed my arm and yanked me toward the steps.

We charged up the stairs and into the kitchen.

Squish. Squish.

Oh, no! He's following us. He's following us!

"We have to hide!" I cried. "Hide!"

Squish. Squish.

"It's here!" Colin screamed. "It's here!"

The ooze creature stepped into the kitchen with one of its slimy orange feet.

"This way!" I shouted to Colin.

We raced into the living room and down the hall.

I ran past the linen closet. The linen closet—a good

place to hide, I thought. "I'll hide here!" I told Colin, backing up. "You hide in my room!"

I ducked inside and closed the closet door. I heard Colin race into my room.

I stood in the hot, dark closet, panting. Gasping for air.

Squish. Squish.

He's coming! He's coming down the hall! *Please don't let him find me. Please don't let him find me,* I repeated over and over.

Squish. Squish.

The sickening sounds grew louder—closer.

Squiiish.

The creature slid to a stop—right outside the door.

I grabbed the doorknob with my trembling hands. Ready to bolt.

I waited. But nothing happened.

I listened. Total silence.

What is it doing out there? What?

Why isn't it opening the door? It has hands. It can open the door. Why isn't it doing it?

I pressed my ear against the closet door.

Silence.

Where is it? What is it doing?

I know! It *can't* open the door, I realized. Its hands are too slimy. They're probably slipping right off the doorknob.

Yes! I silently cheered. Yes! It can't get in!

95

Then I felt it. Something hot and squishy soaking through my socks.

I gazed down—and gasped.

The ooze! It was sliding *under* the door!

And rising higher and higher each second.

I turned the doorknob and pulled. The door was stuck!

I pounded on the door with both fists. I clawed it with my fingernails.

"Open!" I screamed. "Open, open, open!"

The ooze reached my knees now. And it was rising faster and faster. My feet felt as if they were cemented to the floor. I jiggled my legs, trying to keep them moving in the horrible slime.

I grabbed the knob and pulled again. Pulled with all my strength as the ooze bubbled up to my waist. Trapping me in its cold, wet body.

"Open! Open!" I screamed at the door again and again.

And then I remembered—I *pushed* the door, and it swung open, shoving aside a glob of ooze that still remained in the hallway.

With a huge burst of strength I broke out of the slimy mass that surrounded me. I raced to my bedroom.

"Wh-where is it?" Colin stammered from under my desk.

"It's—"

"Here!" Colin finished my sentence.

I spun around.

There it stood, right outside the door—fully formed and bigger than ever. At least twelve feet tall now—with hair!

The creature had grown hair—black wiry hair that sprang out of its entire orange body.

"Oh, gross!" Colin moaned, pushing himself farther under my desk.

The long hairs quivered, quivered madly, as the creature slowly bent his legs and ducked through the doorway.

"No," my voice cracked. "No."

"Its head!" Colin whispered. "Look at its head!"

I stared at the monster's head. It was huge—bigger than a basketball. And an enormous brain bulged out of it. Pulsed against its sides—as if it was way too big for its head.

My heart pounded in my chest as I backed away.

The creature stared at me with its empty eye sockets. Then I watched in horror as its gaping hole of a mouth slowly opened.

"Do not move, human," its deep voice rumbled. "Do not move. There is no escape now."

17

"**L**-leave us alone." I stammered. "Leave us alone."

"Oh, no. It talks, too," I heard Colin croak as the creature oozed forward.

"You have done very well," the creature spoke to me. "You followed the instructions—and you brought me to life. A good plan, don't you agree?"

"I-I don't understand," I stuttered.

"I will explain," the creature replied. "And then I must leave—with your brain."

I knew I didn't want to hear this, but I also knew I had no choice. My whole body trembled as I listened.

"My planet needs human brains," the creature started. "Smart human brains. To give us expanded brain power. The question was—where to find them? Chemistry sets!" the creature exclaimed. "Smart humans use chemistry sets."

The alien creature slid forward. "So we slipped those instructions into chemistry sets all over Earth. And you did the rest. A clever plan—wasn't it?"

The creature didn't wait for an answer. "Enough explaining," it declared. "Now it is time for me to take the rest of your brain."

"Noooo!" I cried out. "No way!"

What should I do? What should I do? Think! Think! I told myself.

And then it came to me. *RUN!*

I dodged around the oozing alien and ran into the hall.

Squish. Squish.

The ooze creature chased after me. Sliding down the hall. Moving fast now. Incredibly fast.

I reached the living room and headed for the front door. *Pull* it open. *Pull* it open, I reminded myself, reaching out for the doorknob.

I twisted the doorknob—and pulled.

The door swung open—yes!

But it was too late.

The ooze shot out a hot, sticky hand and grabbed me.

"Let go of me!" I yelled. The creature lifted me right off my feet. "Let go of me!"

I twisted and turned in the ooze's strong grip.

Tubby charged out of the kitchen—racing in to rescue me!

He ran at the creature. He ran right into him! Right into the sticky ooze.

The creature dropped me as its slimy body wrapped itself around Tubby. "Oh, no! Oh, no!" I cried out. Poor Tubby! He was trapped inside those hideous quivering walls.

I stared in horror as Tubby tried to claw his way out. But it was no use. There was no escape.

And then, suddenly, the creature stiffened. It arched its body, and Tubby came flying out!

He hit the floor with a dull thud.

"Tubby! Tubby!" I scrambled over to my dog. "Are you okay?"

Tubby stared back at me with vacant eyes. The same look Chester had after the ooze sucked out his brain.

"Oh, Tubby," I moaned. "He took your brain. He took your brain."

Squish. Squish.

I jerked my head up. The ooze creature loomed over me.

It was enormous now.

And so was its brain.

I could see it pounding, pounding, pounding against its quivering skull.

"I want the rest of your brain now!" it declared. "I want your brain."

"No!" I shouted. "No! You can't have it. It's mine! It's mine!" I kicked and punched the creature's slimy ooze body. But it was too strong for me.

It lifted me off the floor.

It pulled me up to its awful mouth.

And then, with a horrible slurping sound, it shoved my head down its hot throat.

18

"Let me go! Let me go!"

I kicked my legs.

I beat against the creature's slimy body with my fists.

"I'm coming, Al!" I heard Colin shout. "I'm coming!"

I struggled in the creature's hold, and suddenly I felt its grasp weaken. Weaken until it dropped me to the floor.

I watched as it rocked back and forth, moaning in agony.

And then it began to shrivel.

"It's shrinking!" Colin yelled. "It's shrinking! What did you do to it? What did you do?"

"I-I didn't do anything," I stammered.

"You must have," Colin insisted. "You must have done something!"

We stared at the creature as it withered away— growing smaller and smaller. Turning into a formless glob of ooze.

I could still see its brain. But it was the size of a pea.

I could still see its empty eyes.

And there was its mouth. "Look, Colin! Look!" I pointed to the creature. "It's opening its mouth!"

The ooze creature stared up at us.

It opened its mouth.

"Arrf." It barked.

"Whoa! I don't believe it! I don't believe it!" I shouted.

"What? What?" Colin asked.

"Tubby's brain! Tubby's brain took over the ooze. It neutralized it!" I said. "I bet it could live on only smart brains. Tubby's dumb brain must have put him in shock or something. It couldn't handle Tubby's dumb brain!"

I glanced back at Tubby. He seemed exactly the same as always. I guess he didn't use his brain much.

"You were right, Colin. The ooze had to be neutralized. And Tubby's dumb brain did it! It destroyed the creature."

103

"Wow! Wow! Wow!" Colin couldn't seem to say anything else.

"Hey! Colin! I'm smart again. I'm smart!" I realized. "I got my brain back! And—I *know* what we have to do next!"

"What?" Colin asked, puzzled.

"We have to get rid of it." I jerked my head toward the small puddle of ooze. "We'll stuff it in the cooler and bury it."

"Good idea," Colin agreed. "I'll get the cooler."

I kneeled and tickled Tubby's ears. He rolled onto his back, and I scratched him on the stomach—his favorite spot.

"You saved me, Tub-man," I told him. "If I had a smart pet like Chester, I'd be ooze-food by now."

I guarded the ooze puddle until Colin returned with the cooler and a shovel. We shoveled the puddle into the cooler and slammed the lid on. Then I tied a rope around it, just to make sure the lid stayed on tight.

We dug a deep hole in the backyard—under the apple tree.

Colin and I began to set the cooler into the hole when Colin said, "Wait!"

"What? What's wrong?" I asked.

"What's the capital of Brazil?" he asked.

"Brasilia," I answered, without even thinking.

"Great." Colin grinned. "I just wanted to make sure you were okay."

We dropped the cooler into the hole and covered it up.

We stomped on the dirt until it was hard and flat. And that was the end of the ooze.

19

About a week later everything was back to normal.

Michelle started to teach Chester how to multiply—now that he'd remembered how to add.

I gave up trying to teach Tubby how to fetch. It was hard enough when he *had* a brain. Now it would be impossible. But he's still a great dog.

The other Science Bowl kids all got their brains back, too. We apologized to Mr. Emerson. We blamed our weird behavior on the cafeteria food. We begged him to give us another chance, and he finally agreed.

Which is why I'm stuck outside today studying. I'm spending a great, sunny Saturday afternoon with *Science Teasers* and Mom, Dad, and Michelle. My three coaches.

"Next question, Al," Dad announced. He turned the page of my *Science Teasers* book. "What was Galileo's earth-shaking discovery?"

"I'm sure you know the answer to that one, *son*," Mom said with a laugh.

While I pretended to think, Michelle wandered over to the apple tree.

"What do you suppose these little orange drops are?" she asked as she gazed at the ground.

I felt my stomach clench as Mom wandered over to the tree. "I've never seen anything like them! They almost glow!" she exclaimed.

"Maybe it's some sort of pollution in the water table," Michelle suggested. "I wonder if they feel as sticky as they look."

She reached out her hand to touch one.

"Don't!" I shouted. "Don't go near it! It could be toxic or something."

"Al's probably right," Mom said, stepping back.

"I don't take advice from inferior life-forms," Michelle declared.

Then she reached down and rubbed one of the orange drops between her fingers.

See? Didn't I tell you that Michelle was just a little too smart for her own good?

ARE YOU READY FOR ANOTHER WALK
DOWN FEAR STREET?
TURN THE PAGE FOR A TERRIFYING
SNEAK PREVIEW.

R.L. STINE'S

GHOSTS OF ——®
FEAR STREET

REVENGE OF THE
SHADOW PEOPLE

1

"I'm telling you, Vinny, it was *totally* gross. It chased me all around Fear Lake, dripping thick, green snot. I never saw anything like it."

My friend Bobby Beasley's lips trembled as he told me another one of his stories. This one was about the swamp monster of Fear Lake.

"It stood twelve feet tall—a huge tower of green snot," Bobby continued. "And it had all these long, stringy tentacles for arms."

Bobby stretched out his arms and waved them in the air, nearly poking me in the eye.

"I ran as fast as I could, but the monster grabbed me—with one of its slimy tentacles. Like this—"

Bobby grabbed my arm and I jumped.

"I kicked the monster hard— as hard as I could. It let out a horrible shriek. Then it slithered back into the lake, shrieking the whole way."

"Wow!" I said. I started to breathe again. I hadn't realized I had been holding my breath.

Bobby went on. "That was two years ago," he said in a hushed voice. "The monster hasn't been seen since. But he's down there—waiting."

Bobby gave a serious nod and tugged on his baseball cap.

My mouth dropped open.

Sometimes Bobby's stories really scare me—like now. He tells lots and lots of creepy stories— because he's seen lots and lots of monsters. I live only a few blocks from Bobby, but I've never seen any monsters. And boy, am I glad. I don't know what I'd do if I even met *one*.

Bobby always saves his best stories for after school. That's why I like walking home with him.

"A big, green snot monster? Oh, please," Sharon Lipp mumbled, tossing her long blond braid over her shoulder. Sharon always walks home with us, but she thinks Bobby's stories are dumb. "He doesn't expect us to believe this stupid stuff, does he?" she whispered.

"I believe him," I told her.

Sharon rolled her big brown eyes and nudged me

hard with her elbow. She caught me in the ribs. Which hurt. Sharon is really skinny, but she's really strong.

"Bobby, you should carry a camera with you all the time—the way I do." Sharon pointed to the camera dangling around her neck. "Then we could actually *see* these monsters."

"Uh. Yeah. That's a good idea," Bobby said.

"So, what did you do after the big snot monster disappeared?" Sharon went on.

Bobby squinted at Sharon from beneath the visor of his cap. "I called the cops and filed a full report with Detective Flynn. Me and the detective are like this." Bobby held up two fingers pressed together. "I talk to him at least once a week."

"I bet Detective Flynn *loves* to hear from you," Sharon said, smirking.

Bobby didn't seem to notice. "Sure does. The police really need my help on these weird cases."

"You've seen more ghosts and weird stuff than anybody I know," I said. "Doesn't it . . . scare you?"

Bobby shrugged. "That's what I get for living on Fear Street."

Just the mention of Fear Street made my palms a little sweaty. I dug my hands into my pockets.

"Vinny," Bobby leaned close and whispered.

"Did I ever tell you about the time I accidentally wandered into the Fear Street Woods after dark?"

I shook my head no.

"Do you want to know what happened?" Bobby asked, his voice still low.

I nodded yes.

Bobby bared his teeth and raised his hands as if they were claws. "Werewolf!" he leaped at us and snarled.

Sharon and I both jumped this time. Sharon swung her lunch box at him. "Cut that out, Bobby. That's not funny."

"I didn't say it was. No one ever laughs about the Fear Street werewolf," he said in a spooky voice. "Catch you later!"

We had reached Park Drive—the street where Bobby turned right to go home—to his house on Fear Street.

"See you!" I shouted back.

"Bobby says he knows all this scary stuff about Shadyside. But he makes it all up," Sharon said as we walked on.

"Well, maybe he makes up some of it. But so what?" I asked. "Bobby's a good guy. And I like his creepy stories." I glanced over my shoulder toward Fear Street and shivered.

"He makes up *all* of it," Sharon declared. "A careful listener can tell when someone is lying. Besides, creepy things like that just don't happen."

I didn't know how wrong Sharon was about that. But we were both about to find out.

GOT FEAR?

MAKE SURE TO PICK UP ALL THE SPOOKTACULAR TITLES IN
R.L. STINE'S GHOSTS OF FEAR STREET:
TWICE TERRIFYING TALES SERIES